I0565355

Forward, A Madison Story

K.W. Roberts

Published by K.W. Roberts, 2024.

This is a work of fiction. Similarities to real people, places, or events are entirely coincidental.

FORWARD, A MADISON STORY

First edition. December 16, 2024.

ISBN: 979-8992123401

Written by K.W. Roberts.

To those who want to be more, stop talking and start doing. To those who told me this, thank you. Your message was received.

I

"When are you going to stop living in this fantasy world Theo?"

"It's not a fantasy world. It's the real one I very much live in. You're just blind to it." He felt a heavy breath reverberate through the phone. He knew what was coming next.

"Maybe I am, or maybe you are. In either case, I'm done fighting. If you want to keep living there, you're going to be on your own."

"Is that so?"

"Yes. I hope you find what you're looking for." The phone went dead. For once, he was relieved. There'd been many of these shouting matches over the past year, but this was the first which didn't end with a corrective action plan, nor a discussion of when they'd talk next, nor a recollection of the actions leading to the shouting match. Only a deafening dial tone. To him, the monotonous drone signaled unchartered territory. The support, both fiscal and emotional, from his parents was no more. In the same breath, neither was the necessity to tolerate academia's many trivialities.

*

Of the multitude of decisions he'd need to make, quitting school would be the easiest. His first three semesters of college had proven a perverted academic exercise – absentminded professors lecturing in esoteric tongues supplemented by infinite pages of unworkable problems, culminating in a few exams of which success depended on one's ability to anticipate which unworkable problems the absentminded would regurgitate. Never did he believe his boyhood dream would be abolished with such debauchery.

As a youngin, he spent hours drawing fantastic machines and structures before bringing them into existence leveraging various forms of block. He'd often invert the order: stage a block or two then see where imagination led. More often than not, it led to brilliance. Even if the physical manifestation ultimately failed, the processes brought tremendous joy. His dream was to populate the world with these fantastic imaginations. With each passing year, however, it drifted further away, the limitations imposed by academia and physical science callusing his mind, the incredible objects once springing from it like cherry blossoms ceasing to exist. All that creativity had been diverted to pleasing these institutions and to surpassing his dad, the patriarch who'd served as an endearing, trustworthy example thus far.

A skilled engineer by day and a loving husband and father of four by night, the patriarch was nothing short of wholesome. He coveted his engineering prowess and supported it in every feasible manner. The most tangible support came through planned yearly excursions to a variety engineering exhibitions. In 2005 and 2006 it was the Formula One Grand Prix in Indianapolis, IN. In others, it was the Henry Ford Museum in Detroit, MI, Wright-Patterson Air Force Base in Dayton, OH, and the Collier Collection in Naples, FL. Most recently in 2014, following his freshman year at Wisconsin, they travelled to Western Germany to visit Cologne, the Nürburgring, and the Mercedes Benz and Porsche museums. It was among the rolling Bavarian hills his fantastic dream would perish for good.

Two days of the trip was devoted to a convention in Stuttgart, with the patriarch serving as the keynote speaker on the second day. At that point, he was six years into running a successful consulting company he built following a 21-year career at one of the Detroit giants. He vividly remembered the day of the patriarch's firing in the summer of 2008. He came home at 3:00PM and gathered his two daughters, two sons, and wife at the foot of his bed. The master bedroom was on the opposite side of the house, why did he stop in his room? Or gather everyone in the family room? Something felt different. He then outlined his new circumstances, concluding with his signature pragmaticism:

"Things are going to be different. I don't want anyone to worry. It's going to be okay." That night, tears of fear and ire served as anesthesia, the only time they'd do so for another five and a half years, the streak broken a couple days prior to his "you're going be on your own" determination.

In the waning hours of the conference's second day, he witnessed a masterful oration from the patriarch, one which transformed a normally apathetic audience of automotive engineers into a mob of intoxicated Bayern disciples. Though a beautiful thing to witness, it was the straw which abruptly ended the dream. As the rousing applause concluded, he accepted the harsh truth: he'd never eclipse his success, at least in this arena.

His search for a new arena began with different engineering majors – civil, chemical, structural among others – but all were too similar. He then examined various business majors, but his failing academics would prevent admittance to the Business School. No other academic pursuit he analyzed reignited that childhood enthusiasm, nor did any provide opportunity for superiority. The former realization was another harsh truth, one which the patriarch would never accept given the preponderance of evidence to the contrary, including their recent Bavaria excursion. The latter he kept to himself.

Only weeks into his summer vacation did these stark discoveries transform his sensical world. There was one option which he didn't dare explore until now – writing, the only pursuit which previously caused reconsideration of the boyhood dream. The wrinkle occurred three years prior during his junior year of high school. College admittance the top priority, he enrolled in Advanced English, a supposed house money proposition. Do well, and it would differentiate him from a homogeneous pack of excruciatingly dull bores, youthful precedents to those the patriarch captivated in Bavaria. Do poorly, and at least he showed willingness to risk more than the average bore. The outcome was neither.

His first assignment was a descriptive essay on an event from the previous summer. Naturally, he chose the most recent engineering exhibitions – an American Le Mans Series/IndyCar race at the Mid-Ohio Circuit in Lexington, OH. The weekend was one of sensory overload from the concussing racket of six, eight, and twelve cylinder thoroughbreds to the burning petroleum and fry grease saturating the air surrounding Spectator Village to the violent rain which ended the race prematurely. A young ape could've extracted a decent essay given such a potent base.

What stunned him was not the resulting work but the delight in crafting it. For the first time since his childhood, he felt free as he meticulously selected every nuance within his created world. The newfound freedom yielded an A. Never did he think he'd be any good at writing, let alone this good. Shock, not joy, was the dominant sentiment.

The rest of the year proved difficult as he couldn't replicate the success of that first masterpiece. The prompts of the other assignments were esoteric queries into the writings of others, the same limitations, shrouded in words instead of equations. Shackling aside, he greatly enjoyed the processes, so much that as the year came to a close, he favored pursuing journalism over engineering. However, the teacher with whom he trusted and who stimulated this stark divergence left abruptly, a goodbye nowhere to be found. Damaged and without the necessary letter of recommendation, the pursuit abruptly ended. Diversion from the boyhood dream crucified him, and within the first few days of summer he apathetically returned to it. Two years later, Bavaria would revive this discarded venture.

Upon return from the hills, the decision was an obvious one. Without any friends home in Ann Arbor and three months of summer looming, he decided to return to Madison and write his first novel, dangling red herrings of community college chemistry and working at the Sconnie store to negotiate the arrangement. The tactic worked, and the following Friday he was cruising along I-94W in the gunmetal Porsche 944 he adopted from the patriarch. The small coupe served as a persistent reminder of his presence, as it was the first car he bought after his firing.

Selecting a subject matter for his work would be easy. Like many graduated freshmen, the last year provided a universe of preposterous stories. The day after his arrival, he commenced work: the story of a college freshman forced to relive his unsavory experiences in front of a jury to prove his own insanity.

He thrived in the backdrop of a thawed Lake Mendota and an absence of students. At a minimum he spent four hours per day writing. On the days he didn't work or go to class he spent six or seven. It was an intoxicating, peaceful existence. Every day he traversed campus in search of the perfect spot to fit the story's tone – hidden corridors amongst shady Elms, library desks adjacent to bay windows overlooking tranquil lakes, tables in the shadow of mesmerizing floating staircases. Over those three months, the novel's 273 pages came together beautifully with one exception – it's title, vacant to this day.

*

As he sat on his bedside meandering between relief and regret, he thought back to those days with infinite space for his imagination to roam, the childish block tinkering replaced by that of words. The nostalgia tilled his brain with bygone sentiments as the rowdiness began trickling through the door.

A new era was upon him.

II

With each passing minute, the oscillations between his emotions amplified. What started as nostalgia and relief quickly escalated to agitation and fear. His outlook was shifting. To which direction, he did not know. Apart from the different bed sheets and unadorned walls, he was in his bedroom, naïve, shook, the patriarch and his siblings recently exited.

He soon realized nothing would be rectified this evening. Proceeding to the living room, he grabbed a Miller Lite from the refrigerator before joining his roommates. The can's discernable knock lead into a hollow "Cheers gents!"

"Theo!" his roommate Derrick replied. "Been a minute since we've seen you drink on a weekday."

"I know, right? Just in the mood I guess." He took a large swig before sinking into one of their navy fake suede couches. The Packers-Bears game was on the TV. Being from Michigan and a hopeless Lions fan, he couldn't care less, but he understood the significance of the outcome to the apartment with Derrick and Brody native Wisconsinites and Hank and Kai Chicagoans. These two groups were quite prevalent, near the majority in Madison. Wisconsinites portrayed goofy pluckiness and innocence; Chicagoans emitted arrogance and machismo. Though their auras conflicted, they were cut from the same cloth of basement drunks and rabid sports fanatics. Being a spectator to their rivalry was enjoyable.

"And what mood would that be?"

"Well..." He had a decision to make: completely ignore what transpired with the patriarch, or tell the entire saga of the past twelve months. Normally it'd be the former. Being the youngest of the five, there was constant pressure to illustrate maturity. Though irrational, it'd become integral to his every action. Being irrational hadn't worked well lately, however, so he reasoned the latter was worth attempting.

He began reciting the saga:

"...For a while now I've been considering changing majors and that's what my dad and I have been fighting over the past few weeks. I'm sure y'all have heard some of those conversations. We had another one just now and it ended with him saying I'm going to be on my own if I don't stick with engineering. I said fuck it, I'm done." The room fell silent as all four swiveled towards him. Hank muted the game and then inquired:

"What did he mean by 'going to be on your own'?"

"Just that. He's no longer paying for my school, my rent, you name it." Hank and Derrick were currently sustaining themselves financially. Neither believed he'd ever join them.

"Damn. I'm sorry man. I wish I had something more to say right now. If you need help with anything let us know."

"Thank you," he humbly replied. The volume returned, but they remained silent, their Miller Lite's now lukewarm, symbolic of the mood bestowed upon what was supposed to be an enjoyable night. He took a massive swig, then stood for a second helping. Again he gestured. "Say, let's drink to my problems tonight! Damnit they'll still be there tomorrow!" The lukewarm living room instantly morphed into a rabid arena, all risen toasting to the night ahead. Riding the wave of preposterous energy he then postulated "who's up for Circle of Death?" More revelry ensued. Somewhere in the noise he heard a "yes", at which point he grabbed the torn cardboard skirt housing the remaining 17 cans.

Circle of Death was the group's preferred drinking game. It involved a deck of cards spread around a single beer can. Each card required a deceivingly simple action from the players which became increasingly difficult across multiple games. There were only two rules: fail to complete an action, drink. Pop the tab with your card, drink more.

He set a can on the table and Kai spread the cards. They suggested he draw first. Seven. Everybody pointed to the sky. Brody lost. He slid the card under the tab and the game began.

Twenty cards later following a resounding game of Scattergories, it was his turn to draw. Ace, the first of the game. Drawing one meant he'd initiate a waterfall. By this point he was on his third can and focused on nothing except how quickly he could move onto a fourth. Ten seconds later, he stopped chugging, followed shortly by the others. He surgically placed his card underneath the tab when suddenly, a loud hiss rang through the apartment. It was a miracle the game continued this long, a license from above to indulge further. Reality would set in tomorrow and he would deal with the repercussions then, but for now there was a single objective – finish the fourth faster than a virgin teenager.

In an elegantly choreographed maneuver, he simultaneously lifted the can, widened his throat, pursed his lips, and flung his head back. A cascade of carbonated gold flowed effortlessly as if his stomach were a vacuum. Seconds later, he tilted his head forward to fanatical applause from the group along with a bubble the size of an exercise ball lodged beneath his ribs.

"Kaiser! Kaiser! Kaiser! Kaiser," they chanted. The nickname was derived from his German heritage and a Halloween party when he dressed up as a king and managed to bring a girl back to his dorm for the first time. The start to this night had a similar cadence.

Soon after the chant concluded he heard a knock. His apartment was one of eight units inside a Colonial Revival house at the east end of Langdon St. whose 35 residents were members of Pi Alpha. They were the first unit inside the front door. He and his roommates were closest with the brothers upstairs on the far right and in the basement directly below. Though they had letters associated with them, not one felt connected to the other letter houses lining Langdon St. They viewed themselves as a group of guys who genuinely enjoyed each other's company, not a collection of unscrupulous pricks.

He opened the door to the brothers from upstairs – Seth, Kaleb, Kevin, Nick, and Owen. Seth and he were particularly close as they were dormmates in addition to pledge brothers last year. The two of them experienced a lot of firsts together: first all-nighter, first football game, first time bringing a girl back, and first sorority formal. It was Seth who founded the famous Kaiser chant.

He spoke first:

"Oh shit!" He could barely contain his enthusiasm. Seth then exclaimed:

"Theo! What's up buddy! I heard you were having a pregame tonight?"

"That we are." Seth then acknowledged the rest of the group.

"What's up fellas?" Derrick then interjected:

"Theo said we're drinking to his problems tonight. You better have brought something to help with this." Kaleb, who he was also close with, then raised up a 30 pack of Rolling Rock. They began to salivate. "Quantity over quality, I like how you boys think. Come on in!"

The group was now ten strong, too many to play Circle of Death. They turned to their second favorite drinking game – Flip Cup. Flip Cup was simple: line up on either side of the table, drink your third-full knockoff Solo cup, then flip it over. Slowest side lost.

Game 1 went to him and his roommates collectively known as Apartment #3. Games 2 and 3 went to Seth and company collectively known as Apartment #5. The two sides went back and forth another 30 minutes until the score was tied at five games each. The energy was intoxicating, making it easy to ignore the increasingly volatile exercise ball. For the final game, he decided to anchor, a position normally held by the team's best player. Historically, that person was Derrick or Hank. Tonight though, nothing was going to stop him from leading them to victory.

Brody and Kaleb kicked off. Their flips landed simultaneously. Kai and Nick followed, their flips also hitting the table within

11

milliseconds of each other. Hank started ahead of Kevin, but a misstep on the first flip meant they also tied. The same cadence applied to Derrick and Owen. It was now down to him and Seth. The cacophony from both sides drowned out all sensation. Unconsciously, he snatched his cup, inhaled, then flipped with grace equal to that of his earlier Circle of Death production. His suddenly felt his shoulders being vigorously jerked by Derrick. "Atta boy! Tonight's going to be your night! I can feel it!"

"You bet your ass it is!" He knew then inebriation had set in. Before it became too severe, he urgently needed to convey his new state to Seth. He shook off Derrick and walked around the table. "Hey man, let's talk tomorrow. Some things changed today. Remind me tomorrow in case I forget."

"You got it boss. Hope everything's alright."

"It will be."

With him in trail, the group proceeded outside into an especially cold November night. As he turned the lock, the oscillations returned in droves. Thankfully, they ended swiftly as he heard Owen yell through the door:

"Theo, let's go! We don't want to wait in line!"

He closed his eyes and collected himself, slamming the door emphatically before joining his fellow cavaliers.

III

The frigid night air gently brushed his face as the group walked towards the Double U, the new in-vogue bar approximately a half mile southwest on University Ave. Until now it hadn't treated him well. The few times he went he was either abandoned by those he came with, too drunk, or spent too much money. He was hopeful that trend would be reversed soon.

The time was 9:00PM. Normally they'd be too late and need to stand in line for an hour. However, with approximately 100 yards left, the line was only ten long and the interior only sparsely populated. He thought about illuminating this fact, but suspicion dictated otherwise.

When Apartment #3 entered a bar their positioning in line was precise. Derrick, Hank, and Kai were 21. They would be the first, second, and fourth positions, respectively. This arrangement meant he and Brody, who were 19 and 20, were always following a person of age. This strategy worked all semester, and had so far tonight as the first four passed without issue. He handed his Illinois I.D., Hank's old one, to the bouncer, who teased him by panning up and down then shining a dingy flashlight through the card before letting him by.

Drinks were the first order of business. As the apartment's youngest resident, he typically bought the first round. Tonight was no different. Even if somebody offered given his new circumstances, he wouldn't have accepted the charity. In all likelihood tonight was the last time he could afford a round for some time. Annotating the moment, he bought the entire group Snorkels, the Double U signature antidote consisting of a full Red Bull with a quarter-size hole punched in the side reserved for a shot, or so, of well vodka. The perfect starting point for a night of debauchery.

"To my problems!" He raised the can and guzzled the deadly elixir. He didn't hear if the group responded to his toast, nor did he care. Turning to his right he saw them disperse except for Seth who remained next to him. As he looked for his wallet, the diabolical oscillations reemerged, although by now he was becoming numb to these unpleasantness. The receipt hit the table. $85.56. "Not too bad." Seth then spoke:

"You think Eliza will be here tonight?"

"I doubt it. She told me she had exams this week. I had to cover for her tonight and Tuesday."

"Why don't you find out for sure?"

*

Seth knew of his significant attraction to her. By this point, they'd worked together at the Sconnie store for close to a year. During that time, their relationship evolved from awkward colleagues to trusted confidants. They knew every one of other's embarrassing stories, insecurities, mannerisms, and drink preferences.

The most important thing he knew was the nature of her relationship with her ex-boyfriend. Tyler was a prototypical alpha male – athletic, supremely confident, with a physique only Michelangelo could've carved. Instantly, they developed a shared dream of him as the star quarterback with her as his business advisor and companion as they navigated high school, Wisconsin, the NFL, and his post-athletic career. As their relationship grew, more details crystallized, more individuals, including Eliza's college-football playing father, became involved, and more sacrifice was demanded of her. Between maintaining her high standards and ensuring he had the support to uphold his end, she was decimated, deprived of anybody or anything foreign to the dream.

By senior year, the arrangement appeared solid, though they were now fragile and isolated. That fall, a shattering development came to fruition; Wisconsin announced a new head football coach. As a result, Tyler bashfully flipped his commitment to LSU without her knowledge. She would discover the act during a dinnertime conversation with her dad, vehemently disagreeing with it and the medium through which she found out. Once the shouting match concluded, she came to understand his logic for changing, though she couldn't understand why he'd choose LSU when better offers from nearby schools such as Michigan State, Ohio State, and Tennessee were on the table. Ultimately, they agreed to give the new arrangement a chance.

The fall semester challenged them with him wholly committed to football and her equally committed to early admission to the Business School, both critical to sustaining the dream. When they did find time for one another, it was for no more than 30 minutes. They were trying times, especially on Saturdays knowing she'd never see him in cardinal red and white with the Flying W on his helmet. Whether it was idiocy or pride, her sacrifices made it impossible to abandon the dream.

The spring semester proved easier. They were able to make time most nights and also able to stay with each other during their respective spring breaks. It was still trying, but now they understood it was cyclical. They were even more hopeful entering the summer. He planned to be home for six weeks before returning for summer conditioning and preseason practice. She looked forward to compensating for their distance and exertion during the year.

The opportunity never came.

Their shared dream slowly divulged into separate divergent ones. Though he'd be home for some time, it was now apparent they were galaxies apart. During the spring, she greatly enjoyed her entrepreneurship class and began considering her potential outside the dream. It was then she realized how contingent her future was on his success as a football player. It scared her, and as her dad's playing career had been cut short by a neck injury, she was acutely aware of the life-altering nature a single play could have.

He also had an important realization during this time, the seed of which originated in April following LSU's Spring Game. He had done well in practice and earned the opportunity to play with the starters in the game. He flourished, and as a result had a genuine shot at being the starting quarterback come fall. He certainly possessed the tangible assets, but it was the intangibles, the support of his coaches and teammates, that were proving difficult to obtain. They didn't dislike him, but they were biased towards the legacy George Garrett II who was entering his final year, a Bayou Hollywood story he'd need to ruin.

He left after only three weeks at home to disrupt the narrative. The evening before leaving for Baton Rouge he went to her house attempting to reason with her one final time. He tried earlier that day but she refused. His attempt that night also failed, the discussion ending with an ominous "I'll call you when I land." From that point forward, there was little left of their once thriving relationship. She immersed herself in summer coursework and her job at the Sconnie store. He immersed himself in script fucking. The summer ended with them deciding to move on. Neither were surprised, but the dissolution violently shook them.

Amongst their crumbling dream, he and her grew close. He knew everything, and he also knew it wouldn't be worth his time pursuing her despite his infatuation. She was beautiful, determined, intelligent, and, as of April 14, 2014, admitted to the Business School with a 4.0 GPA. By contrast, he had a 2.5 and was barely clinging to Engineering School admission, nor was he as intelligent, and definitely not as attractive. There was no hope for the two of them beyond their friendship, so he thought.

IV

"You know what, fuck it, what's the worst that could happen? She says no? I've heard worse from my dad." He responded to Seth's challenge with bombastic zeal:

Hey, hope your exams went well! If you're feeling up to it I'm at UU now with my roommates. You're welcome to join. If not, totally get it.

"Done."

"Good job boss," Seth responded. "What can I get you?"

"A beer. That Snorkel was a terrible idea."

"You've had worse."

"That I have." While Seth ordered he felt a vibration stemming from his pocket. "That didn't take long."

Turn around.

There she stood, a muse unlike any other, contrasted against Double U's expanse of industrial concrete, red and black leather, university flags, bar games, and pin-ups in black tank tops donning the eponymous red UU. She looked particularly beautiful tonight, her curled walnut hair hiding a white silk blouse with a tie in front barely covering her breasts, complemented by a pair of mid-rise black leather pants and black boots with a gold buckle. "Damn."

"It's great to see you!" She exclaimed.

"It's great to see you too! What are the chances we'd both be here?"

"I know, right! Two college kids at the most popular bar on campus at the same time. Such an anomaly."

"An anomaly indeed. May I join you?"

"Do you really have to ask?" She smiled before directing them to the booth where her group of four was seated. Three straight girls and Jared, whose flamboyance overwhelmed them all:

"Excuse me sir," he tapped him on the shoulder, "is there room for two more?"

"For a couple fine young men such as yourselves, there's always room."

"Definitely going to need something stronger," Seth quipped. After the pleasantries were dealt with, he turned his eyes towards her. She was nestled against the wall next to Jared's roommate Jessica. Seth had returned and was now directly to his right, leaving him sandwiched between him and Jared, less than ideal given the night's intent. After ten minutes of neurotic analysis fueled by another rapidly consumed Miller Lite, he and Seth excused themselves to the bar. They offered the next round to the group, but before they could finish Jared spoke up:

"Nope. You all stay right here. Theo, lets grab some tequila."

"Fruity fuck." Seth cackled into his hand. "Hey, if Eliza doesn't work out, at least you have him."

"He'll ask you to get Tequila next, just wait." Seth's sheepish grin quickly turned stoic. "You know I'm right." He did.

Now with space between him and the booth, the analysis could continue in a less congested setting. How would he modify the seating arrangement such that he'd be next to her? What was the phrasing needed to convince everybody to move? If it worked, what would they then talk about? Did he want to tell her about the conversation with the patriarch and how it resulted in him quitting school? How would she respond to that? The myriad of questions now flooding his psyche made him wish he's stayed home.

Truthfully, he was shaken by the consequences in the coming days, but revealing those sentiments to her would be catastrophic. The only option was to project the same alpha-male confidence Tyler did. Though he represented many things she hated, she always respected his craftsman commitment to football and the confidence required to uphold his position. His confidence didn't exist, and at the moment he didn't possess a craftsman commitment to anything except optimizing drunkenness.

Last summer, though, he possessed such commitment to writing. It was the only salvageable thread he could find. Rather quickly, however, the thread strengthened, and as if he'd been struck by a higher power, it became the basis for an entirely new being, the state crystalized among the garish vanity. "Welcome to your new world."

V

He pushed his forearm away from the bar's rubber guard, a path to his future laid out in front like Dorothy's route to Oz, although she'd never allow her ruby slippers anywhere near the putrid concrete on which he stood. Before he could further appreciate the road, Jared spoke:

"What's going on with you my friend?"

"A lot," he replied candidly. "I've been thinking; all last summer when I was writing my book I felt...Alive. Connected. Determined. I suppose when I started this year I was hoping that those feelings would carry over and I could regain momentum in school. Instead, I burned out like a dying star. There's no reason to continue." He paused. "I'm quitting to finish my book." That was his story. It wasn't a falsehood. Nobody needed to know the details of his finances nor of his strained relationship with the patriarch. The dawn of this new pursuit called for a mask of conceitedness.

"Shit. That's a big decision. And you're sure about it?"

"As sure as I can be."

"Well in that case, let's celebrate your newfound freedom! In the words of the great Winston Churchill, 'This is no time for ease and comfort. It is time to dare and endure.' Cheers!" They simultaneously gulped their Tequila. Jared then asked the bartender for replacements before returning to the booth.

To his delight, the seating arrangement had shifted. Seth was now against the wall across from Eliza with Jessica on his right. Jared's other roommate, Jocelyn, was next to Jessica, leaving two vacancies next to her. Without hesitation, he snatched the adjacent seat, intending to flow into a private toast before discussing his new pursuit. The fruity fuck had other plans. Before he could pinch the plastic shot glass, a sermon began:

"My friends, I didn't expect to be making this toast tonight, but here we are. It's been brought to my attention Theo has made the brave decision to leave school and pursue his true passion that is writing. I can say firsthand he is very talented, at least when discussing the royal shit show that is the English monarchy. I always knew he had the potential to make such a change, but I doubted if he had the courage to do so. As of tonight I no longer have such doubts. To your new adventures, Theo. May you ride the coattails of Victoria and Winston as opposed to Charles and Edward."

"What the fuck is he talking about?" Seth whispered across the table.

"Queen Victoria, Winston Churchill, Charles III, and Edward VIII. The first two are memorialized across Britain. The other two garner less respect than a Bravo star."

"I get the metaphor, but why did he have to state it like that?"

"Fuck if I know. Why don't you ask him?"

The eyes of the booth rapidly pivoted towards him, each pupil burning a hole through his torso. Thankfully, his experience with the patriarch and roommates meant he was now a skilled illusionist, and he returned their burning rays with sharp ones of his own. The only difference between this illusion and those prior was it demanded a permanent character change.

"Thank you Jared," he raised up the brimmed microscopic vessel. "I know this may come as a surprise, but this change is one I've wanted to make for some time. I didn't discuss it because there were a few things which needed to fall into place." He gazed deep into the eyes of Seth and Eliza as he uttered "fall into place." Their belief meant more than anybody else's, including that of the patriarch. Both of them responded with smiles of genuine appreciation. He didn't know it yet, but those expressions would be forever engrained in his memory. "I don't have much to say beyond that. Thank you." He paused, taking in one more euphoric breath. "To new beginnings!"

"To new beginnings," they replied in harmony. A soft whisper then entered from his left:

"So you're becoming a novelist? When were you planning on telling me this?"

"Tonight. I was going to tell you privately, but Jared's evangelical sermon got in the way. It wasn't supposed to be broadcasted, not this soon, and definitely not before I told you. Your opinion means a lot to me, more than you'll ever understand."

The air thickened between them, their relationship permanently changed. It was established he was her confidant, a role they felt appropriate and mutually beneficial. She didn't know how to feel now, neither did he. With those few words, the boundary between friend and a seeker of something more was broken.

"Well," she started, her incensed tone clear indication of her sentiments, "if it did mean so much, why wait until now to ask for it, in the noisiest possible place, which you hate, and only come because I do?"

"Not everything was in place."

"Such as..."

"...My mentality, my standing with my parents, my grades. That all came together over the last couple days. I wasn't going to commit to something radical unless all the stars were aligned."

"And my opinion wasn't one of these aligning stars?"

"It was. For some reason I just..."

"...Just what? Don't fucking lie." Her attack rendered him mute. She'd exposed him. "Exactly. Goodbye Theo. Excuse me."

He didn't bother fighting. He stood at booth's edge broken, staring deep into the pockmarked table as if it would clue him into what to do next. The dirtied surface gave him nothing except an idea of how inebriated he was as cardinal waves began traversing it, crashing against the shifting black horizon. He finally looked up, his face unchanged, though a gaping void had overtaken his chest.

VI

He excused himself to the bar to ponder where she could've gone. The next round would be a club soda and lime, also known as The Extension, a tool born out of drunken serendipity two weeks ago. Returning to the booth, he turned to Jared for an indication of where she'd gone. He pointed left to the staircase. Desiring not to be seen, he waited until Jared occupied the booth with his eccentricity before slipping away to explore.

*

The staircase at Double U possessed an infamous underbelly frequently used for advancing a recently formed couple's night or as a rendezvous whilst helping an overly inebriated friend. It was the only bar on campus with such a hideaway. If she was still here, that's where she'd be.

When her and Tyler's relationship was souring, she often hid there to gather herself before reuniting with her group. Though he never told her, he'd witnessed her there at her most vulnerable, the cracks in her angelic armor gushing. In these situations, he stood out of sight to ensure nobody took advantage, a rare opportunity to showcase his keen observation skills derived from a lifetime of obsessively analyzing social situations. She was never in danger. The handful of time she was discovered it was by the aloof pin-ups.

He understood her actions all too well. Maintaining an illusion of stability overwhelmed even the hardest individuals. He further understood the crushing nature of having a long-held dream fall apart and the subsequent need to act as if its unraveling was intentional. It was the same illusion he was now performing.

*

Lo and behold, there she was, exactly where she'd previously hidden. He cautiously approached. By this point he was remarkably sober, aware of his recent words and the alienation resulting from them. She was integral to his life, and now more than ever he required her presence to stabilize him. He mustered all humility before gently tapping her right shoulder:

"Eliza. I'm sorry. I know my actions said otherwise, but I hold your opinion in incredibly high regard. I was terrified to tell you anything prematurely. That's not an excuse to disrespect you. If you don't want to talk to me again, I understand." They were now facing each other. Her face moved from being even with his to down and away. They realigned before she responded:

"Just answer me this – would you have made the same decision had I disagreed with it?" She knew how to cut through bullshit, one of the numerous reasons she was admitted into the Business School a year earlier than all but ten of her classmates and why he not only admired, he respected her. She was literally and figuratively several classes above him. He didn't have an answer readily available, but he knew the wrong answers were "yes" and "no". "You can tell me the truth," she sternly interjected.

"I don't know. All I know is your opinion should've been considered, and it wasn't."

"Then, again, why didn't you talk to me earlier, in any other place?"

"Because two hours ago I didn't know what I was going to do." Long, deliberate pauses now separated his responses. "Then I talked to my dad. That was a rough conversation. I shouldn't have, but I then told my roommates I'd quit because there would be financial implications. We then started playing drinking games and I didn't think about it. Then I talked to Jared, and when I told him I quit I felt vindicated. That's when I made up my mind. Regardless, I disrespected you. Please forgive me." Her expression shifted from cold and stoic to uncertain. Though the relief was minimal, it assured if their relationship ended now it would be on amicable terms.

"You're forgiven, Theo. I still don't understand why you couldn't tell me you were at least considering making this decision."

"I didn't want you to think I was weak."

"Why would I think that?"

"Because in every possible way I'm failing. Academically, athletically, socially, you name it. To be honest, I'm not sure I'm a good writer. Shall I go on?"

"You're right, you are failing at those things." She took a deep breath and forcefully exhaled. "But you know what you're excelling at? Being thoughtful, warm, witty, and a fantastic listener. All last year I was waiting for Tyler to listen to me the way you do every time we talk. But he never did. It was always about him and this fucking dream we stupidly committed to when we were barely in high school. It was never going to work, but I was too naïve to realize it. You weren't though. You knew it was heading for failure, and yet you never said anything. You knew it was a lesson

I needed to learn. And for that, you're far more than a friend." He was stunned. Only in his wildest rose-hued dreams would she have articulated those words. If it were an hour earlier, he would've taken her, no regard, no thought. He knew better now. She was obviously inebriated and encountering a gamut of irrational emotions. In all likelihood, it was the first time since Tyler a guy told her she mattered.

"You're being too kind Eliza, and you're greatly overestimating me. I didn't mastermind some scheme to show the error of your ways. I genuinely care about you because you genuinely care about me. Not the idea of me. You're correct, I didn't believe your arrangement with Tyler would work, but it wasn't my place to meddle." He then felt her arms crawl around his neck and unite, then a gentle stream of warm air as her lips approached and eventually terminate at his. He didn't fight, gently placing his hands around her waist, mimicking her subtle movements. This was the very moment he dreamed about since meeting her. He did everything to stay rational during the eternal bliss, but with each passing second his willpower fizzled. Finally, sensibility took over and he carefully retracted. "I should walk you home."

"You should." He escorted her through the first level ambivalent about what transpired. The neurotic analytical exercise he went through at the booth now returned as a furious flow of questions about her thoughts began stampeding through his mind. He desperately wanted to believe she saw something in him beyond her friendly confidant, though that belief, like the undulating cardinal tabletop, was hard to decipher.

The frosty night air greeted them as they exited. She lived a half-mile due west of Double U, equidistant and opposite of him. In addition to the hellacious trek home, he began preparing for the trial his roommates would unquestionably put him through. He could clearly picture the first question:

"Why aren't you with her now?"

He could also picture the crass follow-up commentary:

"How did you fuck it up this time? Did you forget something? Was something not working?"

It would be a long night.

Never had silence been so awkward as they strolled arm-in-arm down University Ave. Usually these moments followed the actions of one. This instance was different; it involved them both. He spoke first:

"Do you have your keys?" Hardly an upgrade over tense quiet.

"I do." The silence resumed, colder than ever, the tension continuing to strain him. With each passing step, the repercussions of harsh candidacy became more soluble. He needed to know how she felt, inebriated or not. He stopped walking and allowed their linked arms to twist her around. She stumbled, regaining her balance before he spoke again:

"Look. I'm sorry for everything that happened tonight, especially lying to you. I don't know what to make of it all but I know I would hate myself if I let any of it ruin our friendship."

She grinned. "I appreciate that Theo. Let's not make too much of it. I too would prefer none of it not come between us."

"I promise it won't."

The remaining stretch was less strained as all indicators regressed to normal. They briefly entered her lobby to warm up before going their separate ways. He tried desperately not to look through the glass after they parted. Sometimes a moment is just that, a moment, rumination the thief of joy.

VII

With her out of his periphery, he began the hellacious trek home. He turned off University Ave. at the adjacent block next to the Business School and began contemplating all that transpired. A few hours ago he was merely a struggling engineering student poised for change at the edge of his bed. Now he walked through the shadows an exile dedicated to writing his iteration of the Great American Novel. Naturally, "what the fuck" were the first words encapsulated by his frozen breath.

Now necessary, further analysis began. First, reconciling the monies. Being a part-time retail clerk wouldn't make ends meet, neither would a full-time one. An over-time one had a chance. Second, reconciling the apartment. Changing residences was not a possibility this time of year. It would be costly, but staying put was the only option. Above all else, his roommates were keystones who'd ensure he live up to a higher standard than his age or decisions indicated.

The outlook wasn't all terrible. Being an academic fugitive did remove the burden of classes, exams, and nonsensical homework. It also meant he could work long hours as a clerk and still have time to write. Not to say other burdens wouldn't enter the picture, because they would. Among the most immediate was navigating the tangled web he'd woven with Eliza. The nature of their relationship was now murky, and they could no longer share in the miseries of academia. The latter would be resolved in due time. Of the former he was less certain as her sentiments around his drastic pivot remained a mystery. What if she resented him for it and how he handled it? He saw that disastrous scenario play out with her and Tyler. He was also concerned she'd seen behind his illusion of surety. She likely had. She was too intelligent to fool. As long as she didn't reveal it to anybody else, it could be maintained.

One final item to reconcile – the writing. He'd proven this past summer he could produce a high volume of prose. Then again, so could a volatile sorority girl on the verge of breakup with enough bottom-shelf flavored vodka. His ability to produce an engaging story had yet to be seen. Not once did he review his novel, nor did he share it with anybody except the birds frequenting the windowsills. For this item, he had no answer.

Despite the tumult, he salivated at the opportunity to put his life's story into words. Success in doing so would place him in a prestigious category – respected intellectuals and writers. It was an eclectic group whose members included Jefferson, Hemingway, Jung, King, and Aristotle. Their legacies and those of other member's transcended centuries via their words. To him, there was no higher human category.

The Capitol's ivory columns brought the analytical torrent to a swift end. He was a frequent visitor now that he resided on Langdon St., but he'd never been at night. Most times, he'd use the half mile walk as a carved limestone and grass barrier to a calamity he'd need to handle later in the evening.

The South Wing was bathed by a mystic gold hue, the Pediment carving visible in the daylight now lurking in the shadows between it and the above dome, illuminated by piercing white light from every wing. The gilded bronze *Wisconsin* statue at the dome's pinnacle stood proudly, her arms raised high to the southeast, the right bare, the left holding a globe adorned by an eagle symbolizing the state motto "Forward". The novel staging overcame him. He climbed onto the arced brass and concrete fountain to his left, convinced the scene in front of him was an existential puzzle waiting to be interpreted, and he'd done just that.

12:01AM. Glorious attainment soon gave way to stark reality. He needed to complete the last ten minutes of what had been a two-hour excursion. Unless tonight was extraordinary, all the roommates would be home, ready for inquisition. There was no point avoiding them any longer. If nothing else it was good preparation, as tonight's inquisition would be easy compared to the ones he'd face tomorrow and beyond.

He pushed off the fountain and headed due north, arriving at his front door a short time later. Even before cracking it open he sensed the unchecked debauchery of an Apartment #3 After-Bar.

*

Apartment #3 After-Bars were a raucous mixture of alcohol, games, music, and weed. There were usually 20-30 people, most of whom girls sick of the Greek's synthetic machismo at Double U. Between the couches and the kitchen there was a cardinal foldable picnic table adorned with the signature white W underscored by a staunch FOR DRINKING GAMES ONLY message. On the kitchen counter, a full array of flavored vodka for the girls and whiskey for the guys. On the couches, a small group usually headed by Kai passing around a bong underneath a light fog. He had his fair share of good times at these events, even managing to successfully romanticize a few of said girls away from the rambunctiousness.

Despite the memories, he'd yet to invite Eliza to one. He told himself she wouldn't like it, that she'd read too much into the invitation, or one of his roommates would say something crass. All reasonable. All bullshit.

*

He opened the door and was immediately greeted with a litany of questions. Derrick was the first to fire:

"Theo, nice to see you again! What happened? Didn't feel like Double U?"

"No. I took a walk."

Just then, Brody stumbled over:

"Didn't I see you leaving with that girl you work with? Yes, I absolutely did! Where is she?"

"You left with her? Nice work Theo!" Derrick toasted before continuing. "You two lovebirds take a long walk along the lake?"

"No. I took a walk around the Capitol." He did his best to articulate the minimal truth, as any counsel would advise.

"You should've invited her here dumbass." This comment induced a slurred elicitation from Brody and the few girls around him.

"Next time." Something far more explicit was queued up, but he held his composure. He navigated to his room and quietly shut the door, waiting patiently for the noise to quell enough for him to sleep. Tomorrow would be a new day.

VIII

7:42 AM. The grey hue casting over his room signaled the new day. He didn't remember how he fell asleep, nor how he managed to ready himself for bed unnoticed amongst the raucous gathering. His clothes from last night were piled in the opposite corner next to the closet along with his desert Chelsea boots.

Aside from the discontinuities, the day was off to an auspicious start. There were no lingering effects from last night's consumption, no classes to attend, and apart from how he fell asleep, he remembered every detail, though he remained in bed to further verify this claim. He first checked for incidental texts, particularly to Eliza, and for unusual charges. There were no such messages and the only charge was the $85.86 for the snorkels, which suddenly decided to make their presence felt. "Oh yes, those things," he thought as they drove a screwdriver deep into his skull.

Sanity checks complete, he then grabbed the provisional glass of water and Advil he laid out, a hack adopted from Brody which proved to be highly effective throughout the fall. While taking the pills, however, he noticed streaks of dried blood crisscrossing the glass. Immediately, he rose and began searching for clues. All signs appeared normal, until he looked at his pillow, where a perfect crimson circle laid, perfectly centered within the divot his head occupied. "What the hell?" He quickly dressed and jogged to the living room in hope somebody could offer an explanation. Hank was on the couch:

"Hey man how are you feeling?"

"I was hoping you could help me with that," he stated while grazing his left hand over the forming scab.

"Do you remember anything?"

"I remember coming home to the After-Bar then going to my room. That's it. I don't know how I fell asleep. Don't know how I ended up with a blood-stained pillow either."

"I may be able to help you with that." He waved him over.

Now terrified, he cautiously sat down. Hank then briefed him on the events which eluded him:

"Kai came to check on you last night. When he peeked in your room you were face down in the corner with your clothes off. There was a lot of blood. We think you hit your head on the window sill. He called us and we helped put you to bed while he stitched up the wound. Lucky for you he had the proper supplies and was able to do a professional job. I've never seen anything like it."

"So I fainted and hit my head?"

"That's what we think."

"Wait, my clothes are piled up in that corner by the closet..." He slowly rose before jogging back to his room. Hank followed. Lifting up the clothes unveiled another blood stain nearly a foot in diameter. "Well, how about that? I might as well leave my clothes there permanently."

"At least until we rent a carpet cleaner," Hank humorously replied.

"I'm still confused. That's never happened, even on my worst nights. I'm trying to think of what could've caused it."

"Who knows? Sometimes weird things happen. I wouldn't worry about it, just get some rest."

"You're right. I'm going back to bed." Derrick then entered:

"There he is! Back from the dead!"

"Indeed."

"Seriously though, are you alright? That was a brutal scene we walked into last night."

"As alright as I can be. I feel fine. Confused, but fine."

"Thank goodness we had a doctor in the apartment." Derrick then pointed to Kai who already had one foot through the door.

"Kai. Thank you."

"Don't worry about it bud, get some rest. We'll talk later."

"Yes, what he said," Derrick added.

He went to his room and shut the door, electing to perform another series of comforting actions before nesting in bed. He first replaced the pile of clothes covering the blood stain and put his boots back on the closet floor. Next, he brushed the back of his head several times to ensure no blood leaked before removing the crimson-stained pillowcase. Finally, he opened the blinds on the lake-facing window before crawling underneath his navy jersey blanket and rolling over in view of the water. Staring through the alleys of the neighboring tower blocks, the romantic days of last summer began playing.

*

His dorm room also had an obstructed lake-facing window, though it was by regal Maples, not concrete and rust tower blocks. During the school year it was awkwardly positioned behind the left corner of his bed, but nonetheless provided a glance of Mendota's calming waters. During the summer after his roommate left, he rotated his bed allowing a clear view of the tranquil surroundings.

Water held a mystical power over him. When he wrote, it was always visible. When he ran, he only did so along the Lakeshore Path. When he flew home, he always negotiated a window seat allowing for a birds eye view of the isthmus from which Madison sprung – Mendota to the North, Monona to the South, the Capitol rising like Vesuvius from the midpoint. He'd attempted in his writings to logically explain its power. Maybe it orientated him towards who he should be – somebody who could afford to live on its shores and capture the heart of a someone like Eliza? Maybe its stillness illustrated the peaceful life of an intellectual and writer? Or maybe it simultaneously stimulated the unbound imagination of his past, the beauty of the present, and a glimpse into the future for which he longed?

Regardless of the reason, its presence motivated him to pursue writing with more fervor than any previous venture, including bringing his impossible imaginations to life. Now more than ever, he needed its transcendent power.

*

As the dawn light percolated through his room, he continued his rosy contemplations, enjoying the silence along with all sensations in his body, including the firmly embedded screwdriver. The sensations soon overwhelmed the percolating thoughts of past and future, only the blissful present remained.

IX

10:43AM. Now occupied by fatigue, he rose, his only obligation to be at the store by 3:00PM for his regular Friday shift.

*

His job at the Sconnie store was one of his favorite things in recent memory. The genesis stemmed from a Wednesday night during his Pi Alpha pledging process. Derrick had invited him over to his apartment following a meeting at the Langdon St. house. Upon arriving, Derrick prepared his dinner – chopped potatoes, butter, and mozzarella. At first, he didn't think much of the spartan fare, but then the conversation shifted to fitness, a topic he sought expertise from Derrick given his aesthetic. The first question he asked was answered candidly:

"It's called the peasant diet. Eat this twice a day and nothing else."

The response gave him tremors. He'd never bared witness to such circumstances, particularly those of somebody he respected. Disgust overcame him. So far he'd proven to be nothing more than a failing, ungrateful glutton. The next day, he walked in the store and submitted a job application.

He started work a couple weeks later upon returning from Thanksgiving. In January, Eliza began working there as a way to earn extra credit for her entrepreneurship class. Her job was to work with the store managers to fulfill custom printing orders and help with marketing. At first, this entailed handing out flyers to the adjacent businesses on State St.. Come football season, it entailed bouncing between bars in a skimpy white tank top and red shorts handing out buttons and pens to Madison's most inebriated, and getting paid $100 to do so. While she was marketing, he was back at the counter handling hordes of freshman girls purchasing the same fanny pack and sunglasses combination, and getting paid $10/hr. to do so.

Aside from this hypocrisy, he loved working there, especially on non-football Saturdays. These days afforded him the opportunity to think and study as the store wasn't overwhelmed by the unstable. He and her also worked together two weeknights after the manager's left. Though they were only two hour shifts, they'd compounded to something of far greater value.

*

He decided to spend the day meandering through the streets of downtown Madison. The sunrise which bled through his room this morning proved to be a red herring as immediately upon leaving he was greeted by a blustering late fall wind. It served as a reminder he'd returned to reality as it foiled the opportunity to walk the Lakeshore Path between Memorial Union and West Campus. The path was rarely used this time of year except by runners and the occasional raging cyclist, the perfect atmosphere to further reconcile his new world.

After acquiring the standard White Ultra Monster and Vanilla Power Bar from Stop & Shop, he plotted his next move. On these days he preferred sitting indoors next to a window observing the city through the lens of a Golden Era noir. As such, he had several locations throughout campus affording this opportunity. The closest to Stop & Shop was the fourth floor of the School of Education at a two-seat oak bench with metallic blue cushions two steps outside the elevator door. It provided a deep panorama starting at the foot of Bascom Hill then extending through State St. and the Capitol. Most importantly, it was unknown to everybody except those who worked on that level.

The half-mile walk ended with a BING at the base of the elevator. Another BING parted the doors at the spartan fourth floor – a narrow landing with a burnt orange wall and indigo carpet sprinkled with flecks of yellow and white, the oak bench in the corner adjacent to the window. He set his backpack on the bench and opened the Monster. The blissful sensation of cold, carbonated liquid cascading down his throat always reinvigorated him. After the first sip settled he pivoted clockwise towards the window.

Immediately in front of him was the famous, or infamous depending on one's physical conditioning, shamrock incline known as Bascom Hill. Lake Mendota aside, it was the campus' defining feature. Two concrete walking paths with overhanging Elms framed the ever-green lawn and the stately Greek-Revival colossus Bascom Hall residing at the hilltop. The iconic bronze casting of Abraham Lincoln in front of the hall completed the postcard.

Through the Elms was the misfit Science Hall towering over central campus. Its haunted folklore fit the gothic rust facade and black-tinted windows making it impossible to see inside. He had never walked in, nor did he know anybody who had. Despite its eeriness, it fit perfectly within the backdrop.

Science Hall gave way to the bustling State St. leading to the Capitol. From here he could observe its liveliness, appreciating its duality as a haven for intoxicated locals come the weekend. Too many times he'd populated this demographic, a fact to which he was especially attuned this Friday. Maybe now that he left school he could disassociate from this label? Maybe so, or maybe he'd become permanently affiliated with it.

The majestic Capitol dominated the skyline. He couldn't make out *Wisconsin* with the same clarity he had last night, but he knew she was there, reminding him of the peaceful life at the end of this arduous journey. To her he toasted his Monster, then turned away to eat the Power Bar which appeared to have been replaced by hardened albino rubber, another gentle reminder of life's many dualities. Compared to other moments he'd experienced on this bench, however, the synthetic bar was a minor inconvenience. The worst of these moments took place earlier that week.

*

There'd been many obstacles that'd obstructed his boyhood dream: none as insurmountable as Differential Equations. He'd already failed once and required a B this semester for admittance into the College of Engineering to remain mathematically possible. The second exam was last Tuesday; he needed an AB or higher. After furiously checking for three days, the grade finally posted as he stepped outside Ingraham Hall, barely over the crest of Bascom Hill. C.

He instantly knew what the mark signified. Just before reaching the School of Education, his world, like the many impossible constructions of his youth, shattered. Instantly, he turned and marched inside, furiously mashed the elevator button, then upon arriving on the fourth floor flopped on the oak bench sobbing profusely, the dream over. Fittingly, he woke to a pitch black window.

He didn't have time to dwell on the loss. The most immediate matter was devising a believable cover for the patriarch. They normally spoke on Thursday nights, meaning he had two days to come up with an impenetrable plan Napoleon would've envied. The initial efforts centered around changing to acceptable majors outside the College of Engineering such as Applied Mathematics and Economics. These alternatives would require additional semesters to complete, an unattractive proposition to somebody already disenchanted with academia. The other alternatives involved various mixtures of university and community college coursework that would also extend his time in school, but would allow for a second chance at an engineering degree, and the opportunity to resurrect the dream. He examined dozens of options the next two days with only a handful emerging as feasible, and all containing the same barrier to circumnavigate – apathy. Apathy towards a childhood fantasy lost to the cruel world bestowed upon him.

This realization finally manifested Thursday night as he squirmed at the edge of his bed waiting for the patriarch to call. Writing was the only thing he wanted to do now. It was the only way to navigate a world which no longer made sense and the only way to create one which did. "Fuck this," he uttered as the phone vibrated.

*

Many reflections originated in this tiny quarter, and many more would. For now, he was content with an empty mind as he nursed his aching body back to life.

X

An hour had passed since he arrived at the vantage point. The time had come to begin charting a new course. Working at the store gave him income and pleasure; requesting more shifts made for a logical first move. There was also potential to take over part of Eliza's responsibilities; she admitted her coursework was becoming overwhelming when she requested he take her shifts earlier that week. Additionally, she wasn't getting paid, and since football season was over there was less marketing. It made perfect sense.

Pleased with his approach, he trekked towards State St. It was here, staring through the mist-covered window of his favorite sandwich shop, halfway through a roast beef and provolone on wheat, he felt the urge to return to the Capitol, though not before he patroned Madison Public Library, another of his hidden oases.

The textbook contemporary masterwork was littered with exposed metal, glass, and white-washed finishes, a refreshing alternative to the brutalist central campus colossuses. Throughout his life libraries had always been a haven, their endless arrays of volumes illustrative of a greater universe to be explored, even if through mediums other than books. Above all else, they afforded the ability to peacefully lose himself inside his imagination. Wandering through the aluminum stacks of his newfound idols – Brown, King, McCarthy, Clancy, Hemingway, Salinger, Crichton – refreshed him, each work exciting him further about his new journey.

2:15PM. He left his idols, their aura invigorating him while enroute to the final destination – the fountain frequented last night. A short visit would put a period on this life-altering chapter. He arrived at the hallowed spot ten minutes later. To his surprise, *Wisconsin's* elegant glow was hardly a freckle against the day's thick overcast, her directive arm barely visible, the fountain littered with fresh white flecks of bird feces. "I should only come here at night." Not wanting to break tradition, he returned to Stop & Shop for another Power Bar and Ultra Monster:

"Hello again sir, same thing as this morning?" The clerk asked.

"You got it. Can't break routine."

"I agree sir. How's your day going?"

"All things considered, not too bad. Hard for a Friday to be anything but good, you know?"

"Indeed sir it is Friday. Excited for the weekend?"

"I am. And you?"

"Sure. Lot of working here sir."

"Most unfortunate. Maybe I'll see you then."

"Maybe. Have a good day sir."

2:35PM. He'd arrived 20 minutes early, a prime opportunity to speak with the manager Steve about taking over for her. After setting his backpack behind the register, he walked to his desk opposite the entrance:

"Steve, can I talk to you for a minute?"

"Sure."

"I know Eliza has been busy lately with school and she was telling me it's only going to get more hectic from this point forward. I on the other hand now have more time and was wondering if I could take on more shifts and some of her responsibilities?"

"Interesting. How many shifts did you have in mind?"

"As many as you can give me." He hesitated, not wanting to explain his availability was due to him quitting school. His desperation was obvious though, and he could see Steve's neck begin to coil as his eyes narrowed. Honesty would be of greater benefit now. "Long story short I'm leaving school but staying in Madison and need a job. I really enjoy working here and wanted to see if there was opportunity here before looking elsewhere, for additional work that is. I still want to work here even if it's only my normal schedule." Most people who worked at the store were students with the exception of Kelsey, the assistant manager. His skepticism was reasonable; normal conversations with college-aged clerks didn't indicate a desire for additional work.

"Why am I hearing this from you and not her? Is there something else going on?"

"No." His next words needed to be extremely deliberate. His approach was going south fast. "I said too much."

"Too much about what?"

"Her situation. She told me her schoolwork was getting overwhelming when she asked me to cover this week. Knowing her I figured she was likely leaving to focus on that. I shouldn't have assumed though, and I shouldn't have spoken for her." Steve paused, his eyes now carefully profiling him.

"Tell you what; I don't like you speaking for her, but if she is leaving I suppose at a minimum I could give you her shifts. If you also do well with her additional responsibilities we can then talk about a more permanent role. Before then, however, you'll need to confirm she is indeed leaving. That's the best I can do."

"I'll call her now." The phone rang. No answer. He tried again. No answer. Steve was now glaring at him, his eyes merely two back slivers on opposite sides his nose. After the third call he gave up and opted for a curt message:

Hey, give me a call. I need to talk to you about the store.

"She's busy. I'll try again later."

"I see that. You should probably get to work." He began his normal duties of seeking poorly folded clothes and misplaced hangers, figuring distance would be his ally.

Ten minutes later, she called:

"Hi," he whispered.

"You called me three times. What's up with the store?" Her tone was stern. One more minor mistake would cost him more than a job.

"I was thinking about something today. Since I'm now leaving school and your coursework is picking up, how would you feel about letting me take over for you at the store? I could really use the money."

"Are you there now?"

"Yes." He looked over in Steve's direction hoping he'd perk up. "I actually asked him if I could take over for you given how I needed to cover you this week and how your coursework was only going to get more intense from here."

"You're incredibly lucky. Because if I wasn't going to call him today and tell him I was quitting, oh boy. All I can say is if I were you I'd stop by the church before going home."

"Indeed. I am extremely lucky. Thank you Eliza."

"I'll call Steve now." She hung up. Seconds after putting his phone away Steve answered her call. He anxiously folded the small pile of t-shirts on top of the register, doing his best to not pay attention in hope of preserving his innocence.

Steve then appeared in front of him:

"That was Eliza, she just quit. Looks like we're going to be spending some more time together."

"I'm looking forward to it," he sheepishly replied.

"You'll start working her shifts next week. We're getting a lot of orders for the holidays so we'll need help with those right away. I'll show you what she was doing Monday morning."

"What time should I be here?"

"9:00AM."

"Sounds good. Thank you again, Steve."

"It's her you should be thanking. She got you out of a shit storm." It was in his best interest not to respond. He was right; he should be thanking her more profusely than he already had. Perhaps a detour to the church was warranted?

Two hours later Steve and Kelsey left. Immediately, he sent another message:

Thank you again for saving my ass, I owe you big. Is there anything I can do for you?

I did save your ass. You can start by bringing me Forage tonight when your shift's over. I also want to talk to you about last night.

Consider it done. I'll see you soon.

XI

After closing the store and gathering his penance from Forage, he headed to her apartment, stopping outside St. Paul's Catholic Church opposite Memorial Library along the way. "Thank you," he nodded towards its limestone steeples, shrouded by the late fall darkness. He continued, the icy howl slicing through the fibers of his wool coat.

He arrived at her apartment chilled to the bone, surprised by his survival. Luckily, the penance was best served cold. She met him a few minutes later donning baggy light grey sweatpants with a matching Wisconsin crewneck, a far cry from her devilish ensemble last night, though it did nothing to suppress his intense attraction.

"You got the goods," she jokingly opened.

"Chilled goods, but yes."

"Good. Come on." Little was said during the trip from the lobby to her apartment on the eleventh floor. Unsurprisingly, the air between them remained heavy. He proceeded to the couch while she gathered provisions to complete the place setting.

"Cold enough," he humorously inquired after the first few bites.

"No, usually I like to see ice crystals on top of the avocado." Her acceptance of his sarcasm provided some reprieve. "What lead you to becoming a novelist?"

"Many things." Like the previous night, his phrases were separated by deliberate, long pauses. "First and foremost, engineering no longer appeals to me. Largely because of my dad and my inability to surpass him, but also because, in reality, it's about finding loopholes. It's not about imagining and building, which is what drew me to it when I was young. When I found out Tuesday it'd be mathematically impossible to get into the College of Engineering, I started looking at other options. I spent two days scanning every page of the course catalog from here and other schools trying to piecemeal something logical. Then last night while waiting to talk to him I finally accepted my disenchantment with it all, and here we are."

"I can understand that. Do you believe you can be a great writer?"

"I do."

"What makes you believe that?"

He took a shallow breath and paused before answering. "Because it fits who I am. Like I've told you before, I don't fit any of these established molds. I'm not an athlete. I'm not an engineer. I'm not a hypercreative artisan. I'm not even a decent student. I'm a thinker. All I do is go about my day philosophizing the world's nonsense and where I fit into it. Somedays, more and more recently, I believe I don't fit into it at all. Maybe that's why I love writing so much, and why I'm willing to throw away everything to pursue it? It's how I make sense of the world, and how I can create new ones that do when this one doesn't. It's a beautiful thing." Both took a bite before resuming the conversation, her speaking next:

"That is a beautiful thing. I never thought about writing that way. To me it was something you did for English class and college applications, and it was always about something you didn't give a fuck about."

"You're not wrong," he chuckled, "I see it differently now."

"You see a lot of things differently. I've come to know that about you."

"I suppose. I don't believe I'm special though, I've just lived inside my head for longer than most. Those who do tend to see the world differently." He noticed she was now twirling her hair with an alluring gaze akin to that which preempted last night's affection. It made him uneasy then, although now he didn't have snorkels and well tequila to calm his nerves. Thankfully, she interjected before he could speak further:

"Do you know why I went out last night? I wasn't supposed to."

"I knew you had an exam that day. I thought it was standard procedure to go out after on Thursdays, but I'm getting the sense that's not the case?"

"You're right on both accounts." She took a sip of water. "I got a B."

"And that's bad because..."

"...I needed an A to have any chance of getting one in the class."

"If you're looking for sympathy from me on this, you'll find very little. I've only gotten two A's in a year and a half." He quickly regretted this snark as he witnessed her expression shift from flirtatious to irritated. "I'm sorry. I'll stop being selfish." He turned away from the coffee table to face her. "What's really troubling you about the grade?"

Her leer softened. "I've put more effort into that class than any other in my life and I still don't remotely comprehend it. I'm not good with numbers, and that's the remainder of business school – numbers."

"I can appreciate that," he humbly interjected before she continued.

"It's not that I put in the most effort, it's that I put it towards something I don't care about. I'm not saying numbers don't matter but they have their place. All they do is reflect the quality of a business' ideas. And that's the part that genuinely interests me – idea generation. I just don't know if this path will allow me to focus on that element."

The air still felt heavy, although now there was a force drawing them together. For the first time, she appeared human, vulnerable, relatable. They were both idealists bounded by their chosen paths. In engineering, it was his imagination by the laws of physical science and mathematics. In business, it was her ideation by the laws of financial performance and productivity. It now made sense why an entrepreneurship course captivated her, and why even if Tyler had stayed in Madison their relationship was doomed.

"That makes a lot of sense. Why don't you change majors?"

"I've thought about it."

"What would you do instead?"

"If I knew then I would've changed already."

"Touché," he muttered as he finished his penance. "Do you have an idea of what you would change to?"

"Again, if I had an idea I probably wouldn't be in this situation."

"Well, what do you like?"

"Theo, I don't need you to solve my fucking problems. I just need you to sit there and listen. You think you can do that?" His body crystallized, his head barely able to rotate. Whether she realized it or not, she'd struck a chord deeper than the organs of Medieval Europe. Choked and confounded, he could only muster a whimper.

She didn't continue her soliloquy and he remained frozen. Their second time entering unchartered territory in 24 hours, this state was even more uncomfortable than that of last night. It wouldn't be the last.

XII

She began to remove the place settings, unaware the depth to which her outburst cut.

*

Though he'd never fulfill the role of an engineer, he remained bound to the ethos of one – analytical, curious, driven by problem solving. Redeeming as these qualities were, they often worked to his detriment.

When her and Tyler's relationship began faltering, he was keen to begin dissecting the litany of information she'd provided during their shifts at the store. The core problem he identified was their relationship's transactional base – the shared dream, another term for contract. He'd worry about being a great quarterback, she'd worry about the business brought to him by being one. The situation was simple, although he never articulated it as such. Like the trusted confidant he was, he kept his opinions quiet hoping she'd arrive at the same conclusion.

With the situation at hand, he stepped outside this role, evidenced by his persistent questioning. He was convinced she didn't want to continue with her business school major. The problem was she didn't know what the alternative was. Neither did he, but he knew the first step was to discover where her genuine interest lay. She already knew – entrepreneurship. The second was to find a path which enabled immersion in this interest. He'd found several – Wisconsin offered an entrepreneurship minor and a vast array of

Madison-based incubators and social clubs. The third step was to execute the first two. Again, simple.

However, it wasn't enough to articulate such a plan; it was his moral duty to ensure its construction and distribution were executed to the highest level. It was personal, a bridge too far, a bridge she and others saw as invasive, but one he needed to build. He'd built it, and she burned it with vile fury.

*

"Maybe I should go," he mournfully stated. He pressed himself off the couch and walked gingerly to the door. She stopped him with the lever half-turned:

"Wait, don't leave yet. There's something else." She gestured her head in the direction of the couch. He obeyed, both returning to their original positions. "Do you remember what you told me last night?"

"Not the exact words, but I remember saying how important your opinion was to me before we kissed. Then on the walk home we talked about the kiss and how it and my other transgressions wouldn't interfere with our friendship. I take it I'm missing something?"

She didn't respond immediately, her eyes probing, then turning down before squaring up. "I believe you're missing what was behind your words. It's not what you said, it's what directed you to say them."

"What do you mean?"

"I mean there's a deeper issue."

"And what would that deeper issue be?"

"You don't trust yourself."

"I don't follow."

"At the booth you told me my opinion meant more to you than I could ever understand, yet I found out through Jared you'd already made your decision. That means Jared knew before I did. That means you'd already made up your mind. You then told me underneath the staircase my input may or may not have impacted your decision to leave school. Clearly that was a lie. With me so far?"

"Yes."

"I believe Jared exposed a pattern rooted in you not trusting yourself. You ask for a lot of opinions before doing anything, even trivial things. The older and wiser the person, the more you ask of them. The reason you do this is if you were to fail, you can divert the blame to the opinions you've gathered. You know that's not sustainable. You're too intelligent. I think you wanted to quit school last year and were waiting for somebody or something to tell you, but you got impatient, and quit on your own accord. The trouble is you didn't trust your decision. Last night you sought validation and attempted to get it by lying about the value of my opinion. I'm not calling you a liar, but I believe you've been lying to yourself for years and its finally caught up to you." She paused, head turned down, nodding in remorse as if she were to deliver news of a loved one's death. "You need to do this on your own. I can't help you."

Hearing these ominous words from the patriarch was normal; hearing them from her was crushing. No concocted half-truth could alleviate the gravity of what she'd articulated. There were no more objects to hide behind, no more lies, no more logic he could use to justify where he stood. Alone, doubting his survival.

"I don' know what to say," he stuttered, "I don't know anything anymore."

She looked at him confused. "What do you mean?"

"I mean...I really don't know."

"Are you okay?" He folded onto the floor and began aggressively convulsing, his limbs flinging uncontrollably in every direction, each a mind of their own. For the next couple minutes, she latched into him like an insect to a rampaging stuck bull hoping to subdue the violence.

His body calmed, and she carefully released, her body in aching tremors. In the violence the coffee table had been propelled to the opposite side of the room next to the TV, the corner penetrating the adjacent wall. She checked his condition. The coffee table had marked his right temple with a jagged crimson line. The floor had scalped his knuckles. The table had blackened his hand. Minor injuries, considering what pooled at the couch's baseboard – a bloody pond from last night's reopened headwound.

She grabbed a towel then carefully wrapped his head and inched him away from the baseboard, leveraging pillows to keep him on his left side. It was a similar routine to dealing with a dangerously drunk person. With him now in a less harmful position, she called 9-1-1. Ten minutes later, the paramedics arrived. As they maneuvered him onto the gurney she described what transpired:

"We were sitting here talking and then, out of nowhere, he fell off the couch and began seizing on the floor. He hit the coffee table hard with his hand and face and cracked his head on the baseboard. I've never seen anything like it."

"Had he been drinking or doing drugs?"

"No."

"Do you know if he's had seizures in the past?"

"I don't. If he has he's never mentioned them to me."

"What's your relationship to him?" She sniffled, holding back her worry before responding.

"He's a good friend."

"I see. Thank you ma'am. We'll take care of him."

"Excuse me," she stopped the medic, "would it be okay if I come with you in the ambulance? It may help him to see a familiar face."

"Yes you can."

"Wonderful, thank you."

They and the two medics were now crammed inside the elevator, the latter having a casual conversation about their child's basketball game. "There's a guy unconscious gushing blood from his head on a gurney and you're talking about Delilah making a fucking layup. What the fuck's wrong with you? Also, who the fuck names their kid Delilah? Fucking idiot." Thankfully, these remarks remained in her thoughts.

She felt responsible for what happened. A ridiculous notion, although the correlation was difficult to ignore. The three of them wheeled him through the lobby and entered the ambulance. Within seconds of the rear doors closing, the gurney began to tremor:

"He's moving!"

"That's a good sign," one of them replied, "his vitals also look good." The other medic then examined his head:

"Looks like he opened an old wound." The other came to investigate. "You see the scab? It's pretty new, can't be more than a day or two old. Miss, were you with him the past couple of days?"

"Yes. I was with him last night."

"Where were you?"

"At Double U. What's that got to do with anything?"

"Your friend's head wound isn't new. It looks like it happened a day or two ago. Did something happen to him last night at the bar?"

"Not when we were together. It must've happened later." A draft formed through the corner where she sat, her baggy grey ensemble doing little to dam the chilling circulation. She was miserable, trapped in a freezer, her conflicting emotions searing her core, obligated by guilt to stay by his side.

XIII

8:45PM. An hour had passed since the episode. He lay peacefully, his chest splattered with several white nodes cabled to an antiquated monitor behind the bed ominously chirping every few seconds. She couldn't help staring whilst curled up in a burnt orange sitting chair on the opposite wall. The window adjacent to her was also allowing in an irritating draft reminiscent of the unpleasant ambulance ride. A knock temporarily reprieved her from the deep discomfort:

"Hello Miss," the doctor opened, "how are you?"

"I'm fine."

"So far everything seems to be good. His vitals are stable, he's had no further convulsions, and his wounds are treated. Am I missing something?"

"No. I'm glad everything seems alright."

"I'll be back in an hour to check on him. Should you need anything before then please let the nurse know."

"Does the nurse have window caulk? There's a draft in that corner."

"Wouldn't surprise me, but you'd need to ask her. I know there are blankets in that closet next to the restroom."

"That'll work for now. Thank you Doctor...Williams Jr."

"Please, call me Hugh." The doctor left and she went to find a blanket in the closet. While sifting through the scattered array of bed sheets and medical supplies, the bed rustled. His torso had torqued upward, arms hung over the metal bed rails. As he brought them inward, they collided with the metal. He violently scanned the room for clues to his whereabouts:

"What the fuck? Eliza? Where the hell am I?" His eyes filled with terror, unable to discern if she was the Angel of Death or the human he adored. With a concerning, warm smile, she arrived at his bedside, beige itchy blanket in arm, her hand gently placed on his right shoulder:

"Hey, it's okay. You had a seizure, but the doctor says you're doing well." Her hand pivoted such that her fingers now softly grazed the stubble on his right jaw.

"A seizure? What are you talking about?"

"You had a seizure when we were sitting on the couch. It was pretty scary. We were mid-conversation when you suddenly collapsed and began seizing on the floor. You smacked your head on the baseboard and hit the coffee table so hard it ended up on the other side of the living room. I jumped on top to stop you, and called 9-1-1 just after you did. And here we are." He took his hand and examined the back of his head to corroborate the story, feeling the fibrous fabric on his lower skull where the wound was bandaged. Its presence provided some relief knowing his situation wasn't fictitious.

"I'm...I'm so sorry I put you in that position Eliza. I'm pathetic." His eyes dampened.

"You're not pathetic. Stop talking like that. It's not your fault."

"Of course it is. Whose would it be? God's?"

"Stranger things have happened."

"Does my dad know?"

"No."

"He can never find out about this. If he did, that'd be the end. No more Madison. No more freedom. No more novel."

"Don't worry about that right now. Get some rest. I'll call the nurse to let her know you're awake."

A few minutes later, one appeared wearing crisp navy scrubs:

"How are you feeling sir?"

"How do I look?"

"I know you're still confused which is understandable as you have a concussion. The doctor wants to come and check on you one more time before you go to sleep. If you need anything before or after, just buzz me. My name is Katie."

"Hold on. I'm not sleeping here. You said concussion, right? That doesn't warrant an overnight stay."

"Normally you'd be correct. But because of the seizure the doctor wants to monitor you overnight to ensure there aren't further complications. You did hit your head pretty hard." Eliza then interjected:

"Is there any way we could convince the doctor to let him go home tonight? He would stay with me, and we'd come back immediately if something happened." She then turned away to initiate negotiations. "He's not in a good headspace right now. Staying overnight would cause him more harm than good. In the ambulance the paramedics said his vitals were stable, as did Dr. Williams just before you arrived. I don't believe he needs to stay. Is there anything you can do to help us?"

"What do you mean by 'not in a good headspace'? He's not in danger of hurting himself or others is he?"

"No, he's just been through a lot. Family and school issues, nothing that would cause him to hurt anybody or himself."

"Okay," she suspiciously replied, "let me know if you need anything." She lunged for the door handle, but was firmly blocked by Eliza's stony hand.

"Can you help us?"

"I'd need to go through Doctor Williams. There's really nothing else I can do. I'm sorry."

"Thank you, Katie." She allowed her to pass, uttering "cunt fucker" as the door slammed. "You're going to be here overnight, but you won't be alone. I'll be here and we'll get through this together." She gently cupped his hand. "You want to watch TV?"

"Like I have a choice."

"Scootch over," she demanded. He quickly recognized the irony – he'd finally managed to get in bed with her. He couldn't help but crack a smile, briefly glancing up to acknowledge the divine humor.

The two of them laid together, hands interwoven in a light grasp. Golden Girls came on the TV. "Keep it here." The girls' banter relaxed them both as they continued to fight through the chaos. It was vital these fleeting instances were appreciated, for it would be a long time before the tumult ended.

XIV

The dim morning light sneaking through the blinds signaled the end of an excruciating night only an insomniac could appreciate. He woke to the sight of another navy scrub nurse asking if he was ready for breakfast. Eliza lay dormant, curled up in the orange armchair next to the window draped in the beige itchy blanket. She moved when the nurse returned with breakfast: fruit, oatmeal, orange juice, and a pan-au-chocolate, all wrapped in plastic adorned with soft aluminum lids.

"Good morning," he uttered to her as he pecked at the oatmeal.

"Good morning. How'd you sleep?"

"Not great. I woke up five or six times."

"That makes two of us."

"Don't feel obligated to stay longer. If you want to go home you can. You've done more than enough. I greatly appreciate it."

"Thank you, but I'd prefer to see you walk out of here."

"I suppose I can accept that. Also, don't feel guilty about any of this. It wasn't your fault. As you said yesterday, it must've been the heavens conspiring against us." A sardonic grin then appeared on her worn face. "Really, Eliza, it wasn't your fault."

"I know. I just have a hard time believing that right now."

The nurse then interrupted and took away the aluminum and plastic medley. An hour later, a different doctor came, interrupting their mid-morning slumber. After the pleasantries were dealt with, he flowed into his scripted questioning:

"Have you consumed anything besides alcohol in the past 48 hours?"

"No sir."

"How much alcohol did you consume?" He started counting on his scraped hand, his shame growing with each additional digit, her expression more disgusted.

"Seven, maybe eight drinks total."

"That's quite a lot. Is that amount normal for you?"

"No. Five to six is normal."

"Five to six is still a lot."

"I'm aware. What other questions do you have doctor?"

"How do you feel now? Any head pressure? Aches? Pains? Nausea?"

"Just aches. I imagine this is what it feels like to be hit by a bus."

"I wouldn't know. Do you feel foggy or have difficulty concentrating?"

"No sir."

"Okay. Those were all my questions." The stiff paused before resuming his diagnosis. "You had a grand mal seizure. Essentially, your entire body shuts down and then convulses for 1-2 minutes, which is why you feel as if you collided with a bus. Depending on where the event occurred, it's also not uncommon to experience head trauma. You do have a concussion, albeit not a severe one."

"Any idea what caused it?"

"The concussion? Probably hitting your head against something during the convulsion."

"I meant the seizure."

"No. Based on what I gathered you have no family or medical history suggesting you'd be presupposed to seizures, although I can tell you your alcohol consumption likely played a role. We'd need to do some follow-up tests to determine the root cause."

"You think I'll go home today?"

"Potentially. I'd like to monitor you until at least 8:00PM, the time the seizure took place, to see if any symptoms reappear. If none appear, then you can go home."

"I'll accept that."

"I'll be back around lunch to check-in. You can call the nurse if you begin to feel any discomfort."

"Sounds good. Thank you doctor." After the stiff exited he turned towards Eliza whose head remained nested on his shoulder.

"Why don't you go home and rest. I'm going to be here a while."

"Are you sure?"

"Yes. You've done more than enough." She paid him a smile before disembarking. "One more thing, do you have my phone?"

"I do." She returned to his bedside. "Call me if you need anything. I'll stop by later to check on you, and hopefully take you home." She hovered over him once more, sealing their long encounter with a faint kiss on his forehead. He laid in awe as she scampered out the room, bewildered somebody of her caliber could find the grace to support the castaway he'd become.

He opened his phone to an endless list of missed calls and messages from his parents. It was naïve of him to think they'd never discover what happened. "May as well get this over with, I'm already in the hospital." He called the patriarch:

"Hi Theo."

"Hi dad."

"Are you okay? We got a call from University Hospital last night."

"I am now."

"What happened?"

"Apparently I had a grand mal seizure. They're still trying to determine what caused it. My body feels like it got hit by a bus, but otherwise I feel fine. The doctor wants to monitor me the rest of the day. If everything checks out, I'll go home tonight." His answer was monotonous and stoic, like a good defendant.

"What do you think caused it?"

"I honestly have no idea."

"I sure hope one of you figures that out before you're released."
The prickly tone wasn't appreciated, but warranted. Any parent
would've reacted identically.

"I'll figure it out."

"Okay. Are you still flying home Tuesday for Thanksgiving?"

"I'm planning on it."

"Okay. Can you send us your flight information?"

"Yes."

"Thank you. I'm sorry this happened to you. Hopefully you're
released today and we can talk about it when you get home. I'd hate
to think it's anything more than a freak incident."

"You and me both. I'll keep you posted on what happens."

"Please do. Talk to you soon. I love you."

"Love you too, dad."

He laid the phone to his left, still disturbed by his current state,
though he took solace that despite their recent disagreements, the
patriarch continued to uphold his role as a father, his unrelenting
pragmaticism rooted in love. For today anyway, he was not
concerned about their future.

Being latent for the past 18 hours was excruciating. He finally
mustered the strength to maneuver to the foot of the bed.
Gathering more, he stood and took his first rigid steps towards the
door, a sharp hiss following each. They would become easier as he

exited his room enroute to the restroom at the opposite end of the hallway. After that business was dealt with the aches subsided further and he performed a full lap of the fifth floor, concluding the exhibition by requesting a clean gown and bed sheets from Katie, who obliged to both, and recommended for her sake he also shower. He agreed. Now clean and mobile, his optimism grew as he turned the television to the Wisconsin-Iowa game and began counting down to 8:00PM.

The stiff returned:

"How are we feeling this afternoon?"

"Very good, though that might change after this game is over. We've been struggling."

"I agree. Our defense has been shit. You could play corner and we'd be better off." The stiff's personality must've been asleep this morning. "Anyway, that's great to hear. Any fogginess, head pressure, or other symptoms?"

"No doctor."

"I'm glad to hear it. Assuming nothing extraordinary happens in the next few hours, I'm confident we'll be able to release you tonight."

"Understood doctor. Just don't check my blood pressure during the game."

"Touché. I'll see you later. Go Badgers!" After the softened stiff left, he messaged Eliza:

I'm feeling great, the doctor is confident I'll be able to leave tonight. How are you?

2:30PM. Kickoff. No response.

5:00PM. The stiff visited and affirmed his confidence in him leaving that night. No response.

6:00PM. The game ends. Badger victory 26-24. Still no response. Though he was no longer concerned about himself, or the team, his concern over her absence was growing deeper. She rarely relinquished on her word, and even when forced to there was a practical explanation. Something must've happened.

Finally, at 7:45PM, as the stiff finished giving his marching orders, she responded:

I'm just seeing this. I'm so sorry. Something came up. I can't take you home. I'm so sorry Theo.

No worries. I'll figure it out. Thank you again for staying with me, I truly appreciate it.

As he sorted through the pile of clothes next to the bed, he noticed the medics had been zealous in their rescue as the nautical colored hoodie and navy Detroit Tigers shirt he'd been wearing were sliced from the collar down. "Fuck." They'd been courteous enough to leave his pants and jacket intact. He rapidly assembled his new attire and departed, acknowledging no one as he walked furiously towards the elevator.

Departing the lobby, he sprinted across the road to the bus stop at the intersection of Highland and Observatory Dr., the pain of his earlier steps replaced by sharp glacial wedges jammed through the voids left by the excited medics. "Those fucking medics." He huddled inside the aluminum and glass shack and began the agonizing 16 minute wait. The passing time enabled his injured brain to return to its normal wandering state. Though not as ferocious as what he experienced two nights ago, his panic lingered, the discomfort of his frozen ribs paling in comparison. The #81 bus then arrived, at least now he wouldn't freeze to death.

While scrolling through his phone, a disturbing headline appeared explaining her absence.

Standout Quarterback Tyler Davis arrested in Madison for Sexual Assault of Ex-Girlfriend

Awestruck, he began rapidly scanning the article.

Madison, WI – Tyler Davis, former Middleton High School football standout and LSU quarterback, was arrested Saturday at 1:30PM at Grand Central Apartments after breaking into his ex-girlfriend's unit and sexually assaulting her.

His ex-girlfriend, UW-Madison student Eliza Wood, came home to find her apartment forcefully entered into. Upon entering, Davis grabbed Wood, spewing lewd comments as he forced her into the bedroom where he began the assault. After several minutes of struggling, Wood was able to break free and yell for help on her eleventh floor balcony.

Davis appeared on the balcony soon after and pinned her against the railing. It was then he began screaming obscenities at the crowd forming below. After approximately seven minutes, Madison P.D.

arrived. Shortly after their arrival Wood was able to break free from Davis's hold and barricade herself inside the bedroom. Madison P.D. first secured the area below Wood's balcony before entering her apartment and arresting Davis.

Davis is currently arraigned in Dane County Jail on one count of breaking and entering, one count of public intoxication, and three counts of sexual assault and battery. Both parties have declined comment at this time.

"Jesus Christ." He searched further and found several outlets had captured the story. Out the window he then saw the ominous yellow crime scene tape and cobalt police lights illuminating her apartment building in a scene cut from Law & Order. He departed at the next stop two blocks away. After a perilous jog through the frigid dark, he stopped at the tape:

"Excuse me officer, is Miss Wood here?"

"Who's asking?"

"I'm a friend of hers."

"Define friend."

"We work together at the Sconnie store on State St. We also ate dinner together last night. She was supposed to come visit me in the hospital this afternoon but didn't make it. I now know why."

"Do you have her phone number?"

"I do." He handed his phone to the officer, who then pulled out her tattered notepad to compare it to the number she received. She gave it back moments later, her expression undeterred:

"She isn't here. I'd suggest calling her."

"Any idea where she went?"

"I can't tell you that sir."

"What time did she leave here?"

"Look, you're not a detective nor her lawyer and therefore I can't give you any information. Call her."

"Understood officer, thank you." He left the scene in remorse, attempting to reach her one final time before the night ended. The robot concluded her transmission before he left a scattershot one of his own:

"Hey Eliza, it's Theo. I read about what happened to you and I'm stunned. I don't even want to begin imagining what you're going through right now. It's truly awful. I just wanted to tell you I'm here for you if you need anything. I'm a phone call away, just let me know. I care about you. Talk soon."

He now faced another arduous walk to his apartment after which he'd be forced to recite a confounding experience to his roommates. The anticipation didn't bother him. All he could think about was where she was and what her world looked like now, a challenging hypothetical which kept him occupied as his extremities drifted towards frostbite.

The front door creaked open to a familiar scene– the four roommates circled around the TV, the table blanketed by Miller Lite cans, a halo of light fog looming overhead. Only Derrick looked up:

"Theo? Where were you?"

"You serious?"

"Yes. Where've you been the last day and a half?"

"The hospital."

"The hospital? What were you doing there?"

"I was IN the hospital you twat." The other three perked up as fast as the fog allowed.

"Because of your head?"

"In part. I went over to Eliza's last night and ended up having a seizure and spending a night in the hospital. I was released an hour ago."

"Damn. Did you see what happened to her?"

He sighed in agony. "Yes. She stayed with me last night and left in the morning." The sighs continued. "She was supposed to take me home. I didn't hear from her until just before I was released saying she couldn't. I didn't know why until I saw the headline on the bus, then the crime scene in front of her apartment."

"How are you feeling?"

"Fine. I'm not even thinking about my situation now. Just hers."

"What a creep," Hank interjected, "people are fucked up."

"Don't I know it. Y'all mind if I join?"

"For sure," replied Derrick. He took his seat amongst the fog, the cushion's depression the only indicator he was present as his depleted brain drifted aimlessly. Away in space, his phone then began vigorously shaking on the coffee table, orchestrating a chorus from the disfigured aluminum. He withdrew from the fog:

"Hi."

"Hi."

"I probably know the answer but how are you doing?"

"Considering my ex-boyfriend tried to rape and throw me into the street, not too bad. How are you?"

"By comparison, good. I saw a headline on the bus and couldn't believe it, then I passed by the cop cars and yellow tape outside your apartment and then..." He paused briefly to exhale. "...Where are you now?"

"Home in Middleton. There were detectives at my house all afternoon asking questions about Tyler. I'm beyond exhausted."

"I'm sure you are. Is there anything I can do for you?"

"I'm sure there is, but I really need some space Theo. It's nothing you've done. I just need to reorient myself. I don't know how long that'll take." He nearly choked suppressing the next agonizing sigh:

"I understand. Well, no matter how long it takes, I'll be here." She hoped the grateful drips from her tired eyes could be felt on the other side.

"I know you will be. You always are. I'll talk to you later."

"Okay. Goodbye." He stared at the pile of clothes adjacent to the bloodstain, conveying his disbelief at the madness through a grimacing smile. "You're fucking hilarious," he snarked in another moment of divine interaction.

Sunday was spent amongst the apartment making last-minute preparations for the first day of his new job and his flight home Tuesday night. His first day would go well. Steve showed him Eliza's tasks and he was able to grasp them quickly. There were also arrangements made for him to begin working full-time starting in January. The pay would be considerably more than what he was making now, but it would barely cover his current expenses, let alone any future grand mals.

Tuesday afternoon came quickly. Though his mind remained preoccupied by the consequences of last weekend, the site of a yellow Madison Taxi outside the store brought a twinkle of joy. He quickly gathered his backpack and black duffle bag, placing them alongside him on the grimy cloth.

Even in the most depressing weather, he was appreciative of Madison's eclectic mixture of cosmopolitan, industrial, and natural scenery. Capital Square provided the modern steel and dark glass, the Oscar Meyer plant the aging concrete and rust, and Tenney Park the amber and red covered lawns. Vastly different, yet all perfectly melted together. He viewed himself as a similar perplexing mixture, although he hadn't managed to elegantly homogenize in the same manner.

A short while later he arrived at Dane County Regional Airport. His presence there always brought peace. A small terminal only 16 gates long, its plain cream and ecru walls were spliced by bright geometries, the vast openings providing idyllic viewports for his favorite simple joy – observing the small twin-engine aircraft carrying others away on their respective journeys. It was a hobby he'd like to think connected him to his namesake grandfather, a former pilot.

After crouching into the Bombardier's tight quarters, Summer Wind began playing. The microscopic relief felt during the taxi ride returned as the quarter swayed and vibrated to the notes, rocking him to sleep, then gently waking him as Nancy ended. The judder upon hitting the tarmac ended his bliss. The trials of home were now upon him.

XV

He stood underneath the aluminum canopy waiting for the patriarch. Streams of leftover rain flowed from above peppering the sidewalk. Shortly after, his family's maroon Odyssey arrived, it peppered by the same streams as he loaded his luggage into the middle row. Following a warm handshake, they set off, exchanging a battery of pleasantries regarding the last football game and the nuances of Madison during the fall, the elephant undisturbed.

Each exchange grew his face longer as the barren trees illuminated by obnoxious billboards of the local ambulance chasers passed. A religiously obeyed tradition for the past 15 years, it pained the patriarch to not visit campus this fall. The past few months had also not been kind to him.

*

The patriarch's father, his grandfather, was a constant force. Adventurous, charismatic, gregarious, and witty, he served as an aspirational example to both. However, the past two years he'd been largely absent, the figure embodying the ethos increasingly degraded.

Even before his decline, their interactions had become less frequent and more transactional. The time usually spent tiptoeing through the garden behind his mid-century split-level or sitting in the passenger seat of his poorly ventilated Porsche 928 was now spent attempting to navigate a tangled web woven by immature pubescents and reconciling his lost imagination. Four years ago the split-level was sold; with it, the garden and majestic sycamore overhanging the driveway that during winter was framed by chopped pine stacked six feet high, became memories. From time to time the younger generations would pay the home a visit to find the new owners had buried their fond memories below a sea of overgrown brush and weed-ridden grass. A special place in hell was carved for them.

Upon his death this October, he realized not only the anchor he'd been, but also how much knowledge was left undiscovered below his finely combed silver hairs. He knew there was more, and now through Eliza he understood why he never dared uncover it. His grandfather would've liked her and the manner in which she exposed him. In hindsight, it would've catalyzed him to explore these depths, a process resulting in a man of worth blooming from a scared boy.

*

They arrived home. After greeting the matriarch and dropping the luggage in his room upstairs, it was time for dinner. In this setting, his sisters could deflect attention away from the still undisturbed elephant; they played their role perfectly. He finished his last bite of lasagna eager for an inconsequential evening of further pleasantries.

The matriarch and patriarch had other plans. Before he could step into the living room, he was stopped. "Let's talk in my office." He followed in anticipation. The matriarch was waiting, staunchly leaning against the bookcase right of the doorway.

He took his usual seat in the worn canvas armchair inside the doorway opposite the bookcase. "I'm assuming you want to talk about the seizure?"

"That's one thing," she replied.

"Okay. I asked the doctor what might have caused it. He didn't have a definitive answer, though he did tell me going out the night before and having more than my usual amount played a role. As you know it's been a tough semester and earlier that night dad and I had a tense conversation which likely induced having more than my usual. To make a long story short, I have a mild concussion and was told to rest."

"So that's it: alcohol and stress? Nothing else?" The patriarch inquired.

"That seems to be the case." She continued the questioning:

"When you say, 'slightly more than your usual' is that three, four, five...?"

"...Eight. Like I said, it'd been a rough day amongst a rougher semester. That's the truth. I'm not proud of it."

"Jesus that's a lot. I sure hope this is a one-time thing and that you'll ease off the drinking. It's a terrible habit."

"I'll be more careful mom, don't worry." Several seconds passed. "What were the other things you wanted to talk about?"

"You choosing to leave school," she snarked. The patriarch was suspiciously quiet, unsettling him more than her questioning.

"Help me understand why you're doing this? I know school hasn't panned out the way you hoped, but why are you taking such drastic action? Surely there's another alternative..." The patriarch then broke his silence:

"...And that alternative, Theo, doesn't have to be engineering related. Since you enjoy writing, why don't you consider journalism, or a major where writing is more prevalent?" Never in his life did he think he'd be the one suggesting those potential paths. He was appreciative, and surprised by his sympathy. However, the positive sentiment didn't last:

"If I did change to a different major like the ones you suggested, would that mean you'd be financially supporting me again? I'm not going to ignore that."

His face tightened. "We can have that conversation when you finish the semester."

"I already got a full-time job working at the store. It started on Monday. That ship has sailed." The matriarch now looked helpless as she knew prohibitive lines had been crossed by both. After more deafening silence the patriarch responded in a reserved tone:

"And so it has. Although I don't understand why, you obviously need to do this. Can we agree to not let it linger over Thanksgiving?"

"So that's it? You really don't want to understand why I'm leaving school?"

"Honestly Theo, not really."

"You're kidding? You don't give a fuck about why I'm doing this?"

"Watch your mouth. Now, listen to me carefully; it's not I don't care about why you're leaving, it's that I don't believe it's relevant anymore. If you wanted to drop out you should've told us why and we could've talked about it. That would've been the intelligent, mature way to go about this situation. That's not what happened. You decided to handle it like a brat, and here we are. You made your choice. I made mine. This conversation is over." He left the office. His words didn't cut as deep as those of Eliza's, but they weren't far off. The matriarch followed. Now alone, he began to wrestle with the consequences of what he'd done.

He fell deeper into the dirtied canvas examining the artifacts of the patriarch's career placed among the hand-built Maple shelves – etched glassware, diecast Porsche racing cars, framed family photographs, eclectic collections of hardcover books, and bronze and glass tennis trophies. There was no denying his success and his admiration of it. He envisioned a similar space for him, although recent events modified that vision to a space exponentially more prestigious – Mahogony shelves, glass encasements for his several literary honors, nouveau film posters derived from his work in borderless steel frames, photographs of him and his family with the stars who brough his work to millions of screens, and hardcover first editions of all his work. He stood from the canvas spiteful, the imagined office permanently etched in his mind. "Welcome to your new world."

He arrived in the living room where the rest of his family was crowded around Bertha, their massive L-shaped beige leather couch, watching the Michigan State basketball game. A different cloud hung over them, a dark one acknowledging the intense anger between him and the patriarch. It persisted until halftime when the matriarch brought an olive branch of popcorn and refreshments. The cloud lifted temporarily, enabling them to converse normally. How long this illusion was maintained would be dictated by the wounded bookending the ell.

XVI

Burdening others with their conflict was unjust. The next morning, the wounded agreed to a cold peace for their remaining time together.

He left Sunday afternoon at 4:00PM. The ride to Detroit Wayne County International wasn't as eclectic nor as symbolic as the one to Dane County Regional. It was especially drab, the clouds blanketing the freeways and the neighboring industrial complexes in gloomy murk, the slivers of greenery and trees between them in a brown hibernation. The murk darkened as they arrived at the terminal, a brief "we'll talk soon" and "sounds good" couplet concluding their visit. Despite its abrupt ending, he felt it'd been a fitting end to this chapter. The next one waited for him in Madison on a navy and stainless steel flash drive at the top right corner of the desk in his room. The only thing between him and it was two hours of wading through zealous crowds of hungover travelers with the plane etiquette of Mongols.

Arriving back, he locked himself in his room and immediately inserted the flash drive. The last edit to his work was dated August 18, 2014, the day before he joined Apartment #3, a gentle reminder of the cataclysmic shift that'd occurred since. The initial pages insinuated pleasant nostalgia from the most peaceful time since his childhood. This sentiment, however, was short-lived.

"This is shit." Three words that disintegrated all joy from those bygone days. Apart from the litany of grammar and spelling mistakes, the story's most egregious issue was its plot – there wasn't one. The work was nothing more than a poorly connected series of embellished events inspired by his freshman year. The more he read the more furious he became. He spent the rest of the evening researching every possible archetype, genre, and style that could transform his dribble into a Hemingway or Salinger work, to no avail. The impossible task ahead blackened the ceiling until the next morning.

Compounding this disappointing realization was a bout of gaslighting. The next morning Kelsey was nowhere to be found. He spent the day scrambling between befuddling technology and unruly customers who collectively decided today would be their moment to bitch. If this was the new normal, the novel would be a ten year project. He left the store at 7:09PM battered, the remaining energy used to prepare an array of chicken sausage, pasta, and frozen vegetables, the affectionately named Peasant Spread. As he devoured his spartan fare, Kai entered. A night owl by nature, it was rare he returned this early. He sat down on the adjacent couch and the pair began conversing:

"I bet you were excited not to go to class today."

"I was until I got to work."

"Why? What happened?"

"The assistant manager didn't show up so I spent the entire day doing two jobs. It was hell. I'm impressed I was able to cook something."

"I feel that. This semester has been a motherfucker. Today is the first time I finished studying before 8:00PM."

"I was about to say you're home awfully early."

"I know, right? Seriously though, pre-med is a bitch. I hope it's worth it. Is it cool if I smoke?"

"Go for it." Kai returned a few minutes later and began the methodical preparation on the coffee table. He'd seen the procedure performed many times as all the roommates and Apartment #5 were regular stoners. His only experience was last year on a Saturday night in mid-February involving a stale brownie, Team America, and shameless consumption of an entire Chex Mix bag. It didn't open any gateways, and the vehement opposition by his parents further suppressed his temptations. In this new world, however, everything was on the table. It's seduction was difficult to ignore.

"You know, I've seen y'all perform this ritual a thousand times but I never paid attention. It's quite interesting."

"Really? What about it's interesting?"

"I don't know. The words are escaping me."

"Sounds like somebody wants some."

"I never said that. Although, I've always wondered what it feels like to be truly high?"

Kai's skepticism percolated through his genial demeanor. "What do you mean by 'truly high'?"

"My only experience was a brownie freshman year and I didn't feel anything besides cottonmouth from eating an entire bag of Chex Mix."

"So you know what the munchies are?" Kai began laughing.

"That I do. What else happens?"

"Hard to say; the effects vary from person to person and from strand to strand. For example, this one causes me to think deeply, so I was going to watch something about cosmology to feed those thoughts."

"It makes you think harder?"

"Not harder. It makes you have thoughts you wouldn't normally have."

"Interesting." The seduction had succeeded. "May I try?"

"You can, but I want to know why you're asking now? I've offered you weed a bunch of times and you've never accepted."

He reluctantly outlined his dilemma. "Last night I reread my novel and was shocked how bad it was. The main issue is there's no plot. It's a bunch of disjointed, disingenuous stories from last year. I tried to begin salvaging it last night but kept spiraling. On top of that, I had an awful day at work and don't have the energy to think. If that's going to be normal, I need some help. Based on what you said, there's a chance weed would help me think differently. If you let me I'd like to test that theory."

Kai pondered his logic, then handed him the elixir. "I hope you find what you're looking for." He sparked the lighter into the grind, the glowing embers crinkling softly as he lifted his thumb from the side intake and swallowed the charring cloud. His throat fought the intruder, retaliating with a barrage of rabid coughs, to no avail. The serum percolated through his chest, spreading to his extremities, lifting his body as if helium flowed through his veins. It was a departure from within, a long-held metaphysical blockade bombed ruinous. "Still got a lung tiger?"

"Barely. So this is what y'all talk about when you say you're floating?"

"Yep. It's like losing your virginity, and you remember how good that felt."

"I do, although I lost my virginity to a whale so that's a low bar to cross." The pair laughed uncontrollably until Derrick and Hank entered a few minutes later:

"I see Theo lost his virginity," Hank commented whilst joining the evening's engagement.

"Yes he did! And she wasn't a whale!" The stoners continued their hysteria. Soon, the supplies were gone, all four paralyzed by the crude humor of the whale saga. Derrick finally interjected after an eternity of gut spilling:

"Kai, what did you do to get Theo high? We offered a bunch of times before but he wouldn't cave. How'd you do it?"

"I didn't do anything," he calmly replied, "he wanted to try it." Hank looked surprised and turned to him for confirmation.

"What made you want to try?"

"I need to uncover a plot for my novel. I discovered last night it doesn't have one."

"What do you mean by 'it doesn't have one'?"

"I mean it doesn't have one. It's a shit collection of siloed anecdotes."

"Siloed anecdotes, now that's a phrase a novelist would use," Derrick quipped, "and what are these silos?"

"One is the protagonist finally getting the opportunity to display his affection for a long-held crush. Another is him coming to terms with lying to himself about his chosen path. Another involves a tense interaction with his father..."

"...Wait," Derrick leveled a sharp point in his direction, "are you the main character in this story? These silos sound familiar."

"Yes to the first question..." Derrick interrupted again before he could answer the second:

"...So you're writing a novel about yourself?"

"I would say I'm writing one inspired by my life, yes."

"But is it about you?"

"No. Why would I do that?"

"Why would you not?" Hank postulated. "People write novels about dragons and elves, why couldn't you write one about your life? Like a what-if story? You know?" He began to analyze Hank's counterintuition. It was a compelling point; people wrote novels about fantastic subjects all the time. Perhaps a realistic what-if story would be refreshing? It also would be easier to write as all the characters and scenery would come from his past and surroundings. These were sound reasons, but a highly compelling third soon became obvious. The whimsical machinery and structures created by his imagination had vanished. With them gone, it needed an outlet. As is, that outlet came from creating wildly provocative hypotheticals which his strapped mind could endlessly analyze. Engaging with them was a vicious addiction: easy to begin, challenging to explore, impossible to manifest. Day-in and day-out they sapped his energy, stopping only when reality provided a more sadistic alternative. Why not explore them through prose? And in the process, vanquish their burden for good?

"You know what Hank, you be onto something."

"Maybe, but before you go making the next Harry Potter, write it down. You will forget that idea, trust me."

"Duly noted." He whipped out his phone and quickly typed out the inceptual plot. "Alright, enough about me, what's next?"

XVII

Apart from the grogginess and arid mouth, the day was off to an auspicious start. Kelsey returned, which meant he was only required to harbor the duties of one, those of which he was stellar. Perhaps yesterday was a fluke? He arrived home fresh like the previous state of his peasant vegetables. While eating, last night's epiphany came to the forefront. He opened his phone to the note:

Write a novel about you writing a novel. It will be unique and you'll have total control over your world. There are enough dragons and other strange subjects people enjoy, why shouldn't they enjoy your story?

The annotation was comically bad but its sentiment was sound. If there would be any hope to this venture, the story would need to be one of genuine interest, one over which he obsessed. He returned to his room and began revamping last summer's work. He made good progress that night and the next two. At this pace, the revamp would be completed on Friday, as with any idealistic home improvement show.

Friday evening came. A dusting of glittering snow came during the night transforming Madison into a tranquil winter watercolor. As he left he felt the powder outside compact and creak underneath his camel work boots, the soothing seasonal ambiance harmonizing with the brass of The Way You Look Tonight.

He began the half-mile trek to College Library. During the week, the behemoth was a crowded, rowdy social club filled with representatives from every Greek house. Most patrons used it as a place to fraternize on their way to Double U or the Kollege Klub, their intermittent studying promoted as sound justification for shameless inebriation. Underneath the blanket of rambunctiousness, however, lay a single row of desks overlooking Lake Mendota. There was one on all three levels, his favorite being on Level 3. With Derrick's Jameson still warm in his throat, he dashed up the staircase, although the urgency wasn't required as the entire floor was populated by only a handful of lonely souls. There was tremendous relief when he flung his backpack on the desk and began organizing his temporary studio.

Instantly, the night's optimism quickly wore off as the siloed anecdotes burned his eyes. The one torturing him now involved a girl named Elena. He'd forgotten about her, for good reason.

*

The novel's original premise surrounded a college freshman whose medical condition, similar to schizophrenia, subjected him to episodic dreams he'd act out consciously. Following one of these dreaming episodes, he finds a girl with whom he'd spent the night viciously assaulted next to him. The girl was a friend of his, Lily, who he'd never thought of harming consciously. While standing trial for battery, he is forced to recount his various dreaming episodes to prove he had no control over his actions.

In another episode, he experiences a romantic encounter at Double U with a stunning girl in his class named Elena. They spend the night together having sex, swimming, and watching the sunrise over Lake Mendota at one of College Library's scenic viewports. After the sunrise, they walk to her dorm, stopping on the steps of Science Hall halfway through. There, she explains to him the night they had was fictitious before disappearing into the crowd of hustling students and faculty.

At the time of its writing three things enamored him: 12 Angry Men, dreams, and Eliza. Elena, unsurprisingly, was used as a placeholder. However, he struggled to incorporate her into the story nee the single episode, yet that episode was a consistent influence. Also unsurprisingly, her omnipresence reflected how he felt watching Eliza from afar at the store and elsewhere. She'd claimed eminent domain over him, even in a fantasy.

*

Each word of the Elena episode snapped a single fiber of the work's last straw, the last of which "fantasy". No amount of editing, expanding, or romanticizing could transform it to a story he'd be proud to tell. With only ninety minutes before the library closed, he scrapped the entire work and began fresh, starting anew with the conversation he had with the patriarch two weeks ago. It was easy starting point given its recency and the heavy emotional toll it continued to impose upon him. After what seemed like five minutes, the librarian reminded him it was closing time. He only managed to write three pages, but it was better than pasting buckets of foundation on a 273 page pig.

A couple steps outside the library, he felt his phone vibrating:

"Hey, how are you?"

"Better, but still not great. How about you?"

"I would say besides scrapping my novel I'm doing fine."

"Why'd you do that?"

"Because it was awful. An elephant shit sized lump of disingenuous bullshit."

"Quite the phrasing. Now what does that mean in English?"

"You remember I described it as 12 Angry Men with a deeper, psychological case?"

"Yes."

"Turns out there's a reason nobody's written that story."

"How come?"

"It's hard to explain. You remember drawing or writing something in fourth grade you thought was great, and then you look at it now and realize it was horrific at best?"

"So you're saying your novel was as bad a fourth grader's painting?"

"Maybe third."

She chuckled. "Good thing you're starting over."

"Indeed. Anyway, what's happening with you?"

"Not much, still a lot of detectives, lawyers, and nosy reporters. At this point I'm used to having them as house guests. Some are more welcome than others. As far as school goes, I'm not doing anything. The dean reached out and said I could get full credit for my classes this semester if I finish them before summer. That was a nice gesture, easily the best thing that's happened to me recently."

"That is a nice gesture. How've you been spending your time when you aren't in a Law & Order episode?"

"Working out and watching TV, nothing crazy. I've been trying to forget about why I'm not doing anything and just enjoying the time away from school."

"Understandably so. I'll stop talking about it."

"It's okay. You're one of the few people with whom I want to talk about it."

"Still, I'm sure it's not an easy subject. Is there anything I can do for you?" He remained calm, desperately hoping she'd offer an invitation.

"Do you want to bring me some Forage," she joked.

"I can tomorrow."

"I'm kidding Theo. You don't have to do that."

"What if I want to?"

"No, seriously, don't do that. Besides, how would you do that? You don't know where I live."

"You're right. Maybe you could meet me at Forage?"

"I'm not ready to do that yet."

He sighed. "I understand. I didn't mean to pressure you."

"Trust me, when I'm ready you'll be one of the first people I want to see. For now, let's continue talking on the phone."

"I can do that. Besides Forage, is there anything else I can do for you?"

"Not right now. Thanks for taking my call."

"Of course. Talk soon?"

"Absolutely! Take care, Theo." In a most ironic fashion, he looked up to the Forage sign, lite slate with black old world lettering basking in white light. "You're funny," he heckled to the divine. Placing Frank back in his ears, he walked through the connecting road onto Langdon St. for the last part of his walk. His conversation with Eliza was simultaneously frustrating and relieving. Though they remained connected, it was by an increasingly thin thread.

The apartment was empty except for the half-consumed Jameson bottle perched on the kitchen counter. The emptiness disturbed him. He wasn't used to being home at this hour on Friday night, another brutal reminder of his new reality. He coated the bottom of his used rocks glass and quickly inhaled, painting his throat with pleasant warmth. "Not too bad." Defeated, he then crawled to bed praying the morning light would soon wake him.

The next three weeks followed a similar cadence. There were only two priorities – folding t-shirts and writing. He still enjoyed the store and agreed to work every day in exchange for taking the week of Christmas and New Years off. It was grueling; most nights he barely yielded energy to shovel down the Peasant Spread, let alone write. The only consolation was his roommates were equally exhausted as the semester came to a close, weed and whiskey exchanged for pots of coffee and cases of Monster. He regularly checked on Eliza, though most of his outreach was left cold, and that wasn't was curtly replied to.

He came home the night of December 22nd ecstatic. Him, Derrick, and Kai agreed two weeks prior to celebrate on this day as they'd finish their exams and he'd be traveling home the next day. It was piously earmarked on his calendar as "Night of Christmas Debauchery."

He arrived home at 7:09PM and initiated the glorious aluminum knock of a fresh Miller Lite. They agreed to begin the festivities at 8:00PM, giving him an hour head start. The first gulp down, he nestled into the couch closest to the door and turned on the TV. The Bucks game was mere background noise to the reminiscence cycling through his mind. How much had changed since returning a month previously. The boyhood dream was no longer feasible, or desirable. That vision, like the choir music echoing from the cathedrals dotting the Bavarian hillside, had vanished. In its place was an aspirational pursuit, one which enabled his fantastic worlds to be brought to life, one which could bring him immortality. The Mahogony shelves of his office began formulating in the walls, the dirty suede transforming into soft cognac leather, his Miller Lite into a rocks glass of Yamazaki 18.

A loud cheering dissipated the hallucination. The next sip settled, then rapidly curdled in his stomach. The curd then clawed its way up, affording him seconds to reach the bathroom where it and every mass in his stomach was soon ejected. Exorcisms sounded more pleasant. Derrick was now nested on the couch in his former position, Kai opposite of him, both staring at his pale sweaty face:

"I was wondering what that sound was. Damn Theo, you look like shit."

"Shit would be an upgrade. There's no way I can go out after what just happened. Fuck. I'm sorry y'all. Have enough for me." He slumped back to his room weakly grasping a pint glass of water which he attempted to consume while sitting on his bed, though his stomach was still rejecting visitors.

He woke at 6:00AM after a restorative night's rest. His bus was scheduled to leave for O'Hare International Airport in two and a half hours. Refreshed, he decided to pass the interim by walking to State St. for coffee. Stepping outside he was greeted by Madison at its most pristine. An untouched blanket of glittering snow blanketed the landscape, the natural and unnatural equally coated. As he began walking he couldn't help but smile. His hardship had finally been rewarded. With Frank harmonizing, he set out into the winter wonderland.

Upon arriving at State St. he turned to his left and noticed the Capitol lit up against the black sky, the glistening blanket leading to it interrupted only by a dim glow of the overhanging white-capped lamps. In the distance he identified *Wisconsin's* faded gold outline, her first appearance in over a month. The unfolding image resembled the night he spent in her shadow convincing himself leaving school was the right decision. To dispute that notion in this moment would've been foolish.

He entered the empty café and ordered a venti black, which even in the dead winter was left top-open to cool as he trekked home, mimicking his tracks along the way. He spent the next hour packing and wrapping the last of his modest Christmas presents before leaving to the bus stop near Science Hall excited for a quiet, smooth bus ride to O'Hare, and an equally smooth drive home with the patriarch. Regarding the former, his predication would pan out. The latter would be a different story.

The bus arrived at the airport approximately three hours later in a menage of sleet and traffic horns. The patriarch's metallic silver Lincoln LS came shortly after, effortlessly blending into the dreary backdrop. He gently placed his backpack and duffle across the back seat, exchanged a warm handshake as they did at Thanksgiving, and off they went. The first hour was filled with surface-level inventory checks. The patriarch asked how life and work were going and he returned the same questions, all of which answered positively. Both seemed satisfied with their respective responses until the subject of school was broached:

"Have you give any thought to what we talked about at Thanksgiving?"

"About going back to school with a different major?"

"Yes."

"To be honest, no. I've been busy with work and writing."

"I think you need to seriously consider going back. I'm glad things seem to be going well at the moment, but I still believe you're taking a huge risk."

"I understand I'm taking a huge risk, but as you said so far it's going well. I'm learning a lot in my new role at the store, supporting myself, and writing a novel which, in case you care, is almost 90 pages long as we sit here. Why would I ruin the momentum by adding school back into the mix?"

"You're not ruining momentum by going back Theo, you're making a sensible decision…"

"…In whose mind? Yours? In case you haven't noticed dad, we don't think the same way. I finally figured that out. And I'm also fine with you not choosing to financially support me in this venture. You don't understand why I'm doing it, and I get that. If I were in your shoes I'd react the same way. Can't you just accept this situation for what it is?"

"And what would that be?"

"Me finding my own way." A long silence ensued before he continued. "When we were in Stuttgart, two things became clear. One, you're incredibly successful and well-respected. Two, there's no way I'll be able to eclipse you unless I find my own way doing something else. Me leaving school to pursue writing is the first step in that process. Can you understand that?"

"Again Theo, I understand you wanting to take a different path. I don't understand why you're going about it in this manner. I also don't understand why you feel the need to do better than me." Clearly, a month apart hadn't eased their stalemate. The remainder of the drive was quiet with the occasional injection of a pop-culture or sports quip.

The matriarch greeted them warmly upon their arrival. Despite their differences, they made a pact to not allow their rift to ruin the holidays. The commentary related to the trip home was positive from both, as was the commentary at dinner that night and at church the night after. Everybody was excited for a relaxing Christmas, although the void left by his grandfather was glaring. Apart from his warmth and wit, there would be no Chateauneuf-Du-Pape, a staple at the Christmas dinner table. The ritual of its uncorking and distribution amongst the table's fragile glassware, similar to the stoner's preparation, was something he witnessed many times but never partook. He would've traded a lifetime's worth of cheap well drinks for the opportunity to share a drop.

The next two days were filled with the typical Christmas itinerary, including a tributary bottle of Du-Pape alongside a spread of beef tenderloin, whipped potatoes, cranberries, asparagus, and creamy pearl onions. The gesture's significance was appreciated by all, but the void remained, each sip increasing its already vast expanse. That night lying in bed, he thought deeply about what his grandfather would say to him now. He couldn't muster a single sentence, only deeper hatred towards himself and his lack of exploration. In his rage, he then remembered his experience last month and the metaphysical barriers he was able to transcend. The potential to do so again quelled the rage. As far as acting on this potential, his old friend Kristoff might be of service.

*

Him and Kristoff's relationship began the summer before his freshman year of high school at tennis tryouts when the two unexpectedly bonded. Kristoff was a senior and allowed him to tag along with him and his friends during the summer and gave him rides home after practice when school began. Most importantly, he provided a necessary example for him to follow as he navigated the pitfalls of high school, offering a glimpse of what life should resemble in three years.

After tennis season ended in the fall, the two wouldn't see each other for the next few years despite Kristoff attending the University of Michigan. They finally reconnected last winter after his first semester at Wisconsin and now met regularly when they were in Ann Arbor. Despite their reconnection, he believed another year or two of his guidance would've steered him differently, another challenging hypothetical he couldn't help but ponder.

*

Unable to fall asleep, he messaged him in hope he'd have weed. He did, and agreed to meet him tomorrow over lunch at Knight's to give it to him.

They met at 12:30PM. Knight's was a classic steakhouse, its interior a gilded melting pot of beige and white framed by Walnut trim, the bar filled with bottles of Whiskey worth more than his rent. The elitism saturated him as the maître d' led them to their table. As with most of their meetings, the opening dialogue was filled with reminiscences about their hometown and high school, a mutual dislike of the former and latter affording several bonding moments, though today these grovels didn't seem necessary. They'd lived away long enough to see this time as a necessary stepping stone. Unconsciously, they knew these grovels were what ultimately pushed them beyond. They wouldn't have had it any other way.

They finished the meal in silence, him speaking first after their plates cleared:

"Did I tell you I'm writing a book?"

"No shit. Trying to be the next Hemingway are you?"

"More like Stephen King, but Ernest isn't a bad goal."

"What's it about?"

"It's about a college sophomore whose disenchantment leads him to quit school and write a book. Think Catcher in the Rye set in present day Madison, and Holden is in college. I started a different story last summer, which was a horrific psychological variation of 12 Angry Men, scrapped it a month ago, started fresh, and now have almost 100 pages as we sit here."

"Damn, 100 pages is progress. Where's it going?"

"You mean what's the ending?"

"No. The plot. What challenges does the protagonist face? What journey does he go on?"

"So far he's faced disapproval from his father, a complicated romantic relationship, and the realities of being a semi-starving artist. He's now beginning to accept his new world and is on the verge of thriving in it."

"Interesting," Kristoff responded in an off-putting tone.

"I think so."

"If you don't mind me asking, if this novel is centered around a disenchanted college sophomore, how close is it to being a true story?" He paused before answering. Kristoff was a dear friend deserving of the unadulterated truth. He suspended the remnants of his Old Fashioned between the table and him, answering deliberately:

"95%."

"What's the 5% which isn't?"

"Some of the dialogue isn't verbatim because I couldn't remember the exact words, only the sentiment associated with them. Some of the timeline is off for the same reason..."

"...But the characters, emotions, events, that's all true?"

"Yes."

"So as we sit here, you're a college dropout writing a semi-autobiographical novel about you dropping out of college to write a novel?"

"Precisely." A longer pause ensued with his eyes fixated on Kristoff, whose eyes were fixated on the muddled carcass in his glass. He then gestured a toast:

"My friend, you got some serious chutzpa. I'm rooting for you to figure it out."

"I appreciate that." They clinked glasses and heckled the waiter for another round.

"Do you feel liberated now that you've decided to take the path of artistic suffering?"

"In some ways, but overall I'm still adjusting. I continue to struggle with nobody understanding why I'm doing what I'm doing."

"That'll come with time. Lucky for me I have the luxury of older siblings who are doctors and who've already exceeded my parent's expectations, including giving them five grandchildren. As long as I'm not in jail I'm doing well."

"Must be nice." The next Old Fashioneds then arrived. They were quickly polished off and the two left Knight's for a coffee shop next door. After ordering a pair of double espressos, they found a table next to the window where the inquiries resumed:

"If you are going to be the next Stephen King, can I assume you have a more ideas than this self-fulfilling prophecy?" His pious phrasing managed to lighten even the most daunting questions.

"I do. The story I'm writing now is the first of a trilogy. The next book will be about him writing a second novel amongst increasingly complicated personal circumstances. The final one will be about eliminating those complexities and finding balance in his life whilst writing his third novel." He stopped, sensing an epiphanous moment coming. "I suppose that's where this is going." The last sip of lukewarm espresso trickled down his raspy throat. "Beyond that, I have several ideas for historical fiction books, a crime thriller and science-fiction series which I'd want to make into a TV show and a film, respectively. I also have a drama series that'd be written in tandem with a TV show."

"That's quite a map you've drawn. I appreciate there aren't any plans to write about savage pets or demented clowns."

"You and me both. I'm striving for Different Seasons as opposed to It." Kristoff chuckled then finished his lukewarm concentrate.

"Returning to the current trilogy, what's your character going to face in the next book? That'll help you write this one."

"In addition to writing his second novel, he must further reconcile his successful rebellion with his underlying desire to please his family. Additionally, his love interest plays a different role than when she was a conquest which creates significant tension between them. Furthermore, in the background of these storylines are his personal demons that begin to emerge with great force. Some he conquers, some he doesn't."

"And the next book?"

"He finds peace. He learns to appreciate the journey and his newly forged role."

"That of a storyteller?"

"Exactly." The epiphany arrived. "Another shot?"

"Sure." He returned with two miniature porcelain mugs. "Prost!" They lifted the steaming updraft in tribute to his high ambitions.

XVIII

He never asked Kristoff. It would've been inappropriate given the guidance he provided not just that afternoon but back in his teenage years. He was a sherpa, not a plug.

New Years Day came and went and he drove back to Madison with the patriarch on January 2, 2015. The conversation this trip was similar to the one before Christmas, though they avoided the subject of school and his work like the plague. A ceasefire was in place, neither side desiring to break it. He was happy when the final pleasantries were exchanged and he could be alone amongst the vacant apartment. A depressing site two weeks earlier, it now invigorated him with creativity. He fixed a large pot of coffee, set up at the kitchen counter, and took the novel beyond the 100-page mark.

The next couple of weeks proved productive. January was a slow time at the store, affording the energy to capitalize on working several extra shifts. Often he'd bring his laptop to squeeze in extra words when Steve and Kelsey weren't there, or weren't looking. January was an equally slow month for the city of Madison. The absence of raucous students brought a calm mimicking the atmosphere of the summer months. After work he frequently took the extended route home around the Capitol passing Madison Public Library and the fountain. *Wisconsin's* glow had returned, every pass in her shadow additional assurance his ambitious pursuits would prove fruitful.

Him and Eliza only spoke New Years Eve, her absence a glaring blemish in an otherwise picturesque start to the new year. He began to believe, like the protagonist in his original novel, his relationship with her was nothing more than a dream. At least for now, it was easier to accept she'd vanished like the steam vapors from him and Kristoff's cooling espressos.

Derrick returned Friday, January 16th. He was excited to see him. As much as he enjoyed having the apartment to himself, it was a big space for a sole burgeoning writer. After work, he walked in to find him on the couch, Miller Lite in hand:

"Should we pick up where we left off?"

"What do you mean?"

"We were supposed to go out the night you finished exams. Unfortunately, my stomach had other ideas."

"Oh yes, forgot about that. I wasn't planning on going out tonight, but I suppose we could."

"What were you planning on doing?"

"Getting high. Nobody's back."

"That sounds equally appealing. You mind if I join?"

"If you promise to be as funny as last time."

"I'll do my best." His excitement grew as Derrick prepared the leafy tonic. It'd been over a month since that first experience and he'd been looking forward to another given the strain of recent writing sessions. His story was at a crossroads, the chosen direction potentially imparting severe consequences on the trilogy. He enthusiastically took the first hit hopeful psychedelic insight would guide him wisely.

Light coughing subdued, it was apparent this experience wouldn't be like the last. Instead of a lifted burden, a severe one leaped onto his back, the sharpened attention and lightness from last time nowhere in sight. Suddenly, the thematic conversation with Kristoff about the trilogy and his future endeavors struck like a commandment, the consequences of rebellion alluded to by the patriarch a deafening symphony bursting through the walls, Eliza's ghost forming and disintegrating in the wispy cloud. He was spiraling down a rabbit hole shackled to the suede, the only remedy to grip the adjacent cushions as if death a slip away.

12:15AM. He was alone. Understanding what could've happened, he immediately rose from the suede and began investigating. All furniture was where it started. Check. No blood. Check. No aches, bruises, or bumps. Check. Empty Miller Lite cans dusted with burnt grass. Check. He walked to his room and resumed his slumber.

Morning came and the apartment was once again empty nee the remnants of last night's supplies left unaltered on the table's left edge. He stared at them cynically through swollen eyes, for he now understood the duopoly within the leaves. Electing not to revisit the tortuous thoughts he encountered last night, he proceeded with his normal routine enroute to the store. His shift that day and the next were particularly slow, which would've been enjoyable had he been present. His eyes were 35mm projectors rotating at half speed, him forgetful of everything, his movements arduous and slow. Folding t-shirts was a herculean task. He wasn't sure how two days had passed by the time his shift on Sunday ended at 6:00PM.

With the student population back on campus, his world was once again crowded with nagging reminders of the past. In the following week he managed to encounter Seth, Kaleb, Kevin, Nick, and Owen, all of whom he hadn't seen since that fateful night at Double U. They all wanted to know what happened, especially Seth, who now had two classes with Jared. Besides that comedic irony, little else brough him joy during the winter.

The second week of March brought with it unseasonably warm weather, above 40 degrees Fahrenheit. He came home Friday, March 13th, excited by the emerging spring, the last piles of snow receding to their mossy undergrowth. The early stages of a classic Apartment #3 pregame were in full swing. "When in Rome." He prepared a glass of ice and Wild Turkey 101, his new drink of choice, and joined the infant party.

He'd forgotten how entertaining they were, and how they were a rare instance he felt part of something significant, even if it was drunkenness. An hour in, courtesy of copious 101, he was transported back to the first party they had in August, lost in the bass billowing from their recently purchased loudspeaker. He poured himself another glass. Returning to the festivities, he noticed an unfamiliar muse in a satin black strapless romper leaning against the couch staring at him through luscious hazel eyes, her cleavage a deep ravine. He returned her stare and approached:

"You seem lonely," he opened confidently.

"Not really, but I am thirsty. What do you have there?"

"Bourbon. Would you like some?"

"If you're offering."

He then gestured towards the bar like a pretentious butler school dropout. "Right this way." The unfamiliar muse sat down and watched him fill the glass with ice. "Wait, you didn't ask if I wanted it neat or on the rocks."

"You're absolutely right. Would you like it neat or on the rocks?"

"On the rocks. It's 101." He finished bartending then started to hand her the drink before stopping. She gave him a playful smirk. "What now?"

"You never told me your name."

"It's Nikki. Can I have my drink?"

"You're not going to ask what mine is?" He devilishly swirled the glass in her face, strategically blocking his view of the ravine.

"Fine. What's your name?"

"Theo." He handed her the 101 and toasted. "To new friends!"

"And shit bartenders!"

Nikki was a short, barely five foot brunette who was part of the Jewish sorority two blocks away next to the lake. Cute, sassy, and a lover of bourbon, she embodied three traits especially attractive to him tonight. They continued their banter about him speaking in a fake British accent and how she could be in a Jewish sorority if she wasn't Jewish or from New York, to which she replied "I got tits and a 4.0. They call me the Equalizer." He couldn't help but laugh hysterically.

"So, Equalizer, what brought you to Madison?"

"School."

"Okay yes. What school specifically?"

"Medical school, hopefully."

"That's very admirable. Why are you pursuing it?"

"I've always wanted to help people, plus I'm really good at science, especially anatomy and chemistry. Just made sense. What about you? What brought you here?"

"Initially, engineering, but it wasn't what I thought it'd be. I actually don't have a major right now."

"Don't you have to figure that out soon?"

"If I was in school I would."

"So you're not in school but living on campus with a bunch of guys?"

"Precisely."

"So what's your plan? I'm sorry, I probably sound like your mother. Forget I said that."

"No it's fine. I work at the Sconnie store full time and am writing a novel, hence why I'm good at drinking bourbon."

"That's admirable in its own way. What do your parents think about what you're doing?"

"They think it's a phase."

"Is it?"

"No. It's permanent. I've been on my own since November. No school. No financial support. Nothing. All in the pursuit of writing. January and February were awful. It was as if every day I'd encounter somebody I know doing 'normal' college things while I'm off working seven days a week and writing at night. I learned then the universe is quite sadistic. You think I'd be numb to it after four months, but I'm not."

"I know how you feel. Studying for the MCAT is that way. It's every day and night. All my friends are watching The Bachelorette and drinking Yellowtail and I'm heading out the door like 'wish I could be basic with y'all, but I have to bang my head against this prep book for three hours.'"

"Amen to that." He was enjoying their conversation, sensing the threads of a connection weaving, desiring to slip away and continue their evening alone. He leaned in closer. "It's getting loud and my throat feels like I smoked a carton of Marlboros. Do you want to go someplace quieter and talk?"

"I do."

"My room's down that hall." The two of them slithered away. They sat down at the edge of the bed lustfully staring at each other. In that moment, they mutually agreed their conversation had ended. They started kissing, stripping, trading positions with great agility, the closest scene to passionate Hollywood sex either had experienced. The pair briefly settled before she ripped off his boxers and started blowing him. He wasn't sure if he was dreaming. He didn't care.

His phone then vibrated loudly on the nightstand. He ignored it at first, but then it persisted two more times. He reached for it, interrupting her work in the process. Three messages from Eliza.

"Everything okay?" He suddenly became overrun with guilt, the burden as crippling as that of last week's trip. Though they were not together, she maintained powerful domain.

"Yes. As you were." She continued. The sensation was incredible, though his mind was now elsewhere. Not even heavenly oral sex could break her grip. "Nikki, I'm sorry, I can't do this with you. It wouldn't be fair."

"What do you mean? You're not cheating on somebody are you?!?"

"No. A good friend of mine is going through a lot and she messaged me. I'm sorry. It's got nothing to do with you."

"She? Good friend my fucking ass." She got dressed and exited in a fit of rage. He felt it best to remain silent.

After redressing he read the messages:

Hey, I'm really sorry I haven't reached out. I'm not ignoring you, it's just been crazy while this is getting sorted. The justice system isn't in my house anymore which is nice, but it's still overwhelming.

I'm coming downtown tomorrow for a charity spin class. I'd love for you to join. I'll pay for your ticket.

Let me know tonight if you can make it!

He was ecstatic, finishing the 101 before lying down and compiling his sentiments. The noise from the pregame soon ended, but the night was far from over. Shortly after the apartment emptied a titan began crushing his stomach as if its leg were being amputated. Before he could think, he was crouched on the bathroom floor, praying to the porcelain goddess.

The worst part about zealous drinking was the severe dizziness colloquially referred to as the spins. The ones he was experiencing now were the worst he'd ever encountered. It took a massive effort to rise and stumble to his room where the titan then impatiently ordered him back for more prayer. After this penance, he curled up alongside the porcelain, like he should've been with Nikki. Eventually and with great clumsiness, he crawled across the hall, kicking the door closed as he dived on his bed.

9:30AM. The penetrating morning light brought with it a tsunami of excruciating pain. He could barely move, his head pounded against an anvil, unable to recall much about his escapades other than they didn't end well. He did remember Eliza texted him, and that he also forgot to confirm he'd be at her class. He panicked and immediately messaged her:

I'm sorry I didn't get back to you last night. I'd love to go. What time is the class?

She quickly replied:

It's at 1 at Cyc on University, above Fresh Market. I'll go ahead and sign you up. Looking forward to seeing you!

With that excitement out of the way, he turned his attention back to the 101-inflicted agony. He knew a serious remedy would be required to make even the most begrudged appearance. Aspirin and water in mass came first, then coffee, in greater mass, then whatever food could be kept down. The first two stages went smoothly, but his stomach valiantly fought the third until it was time to leave at 12:30PM.

He marched in hallucination fueled by nothing except a burning desire to see her and a crab pot of coffee. Death would've felt better, but every step gifted him just enough strength to take another, a heroic display, indistinguishable from Maximus in his eyes, indistinguishable from a walk of shame in everyone else's. Arriving 15 minutes later, he immediately spotted her skin-tight black ensemble complemented by an equally tight low ponytail. The throbbing rapidly dissolved. "Damn."

It returned just as rapidly, however, upon the site of Jessica and Jocelyn next to her. "Fuck." Yet another obstacle he'd need to overcome. He didn't like either, and they didn't like him, both seeing the other as a perennial third wheel. He wasn't going to allow them to sully a heroic march, albeit one initiated by his own incompetence.

One step, then the instructor, Jared, made an announcement:

"Hello everyone! I want to start off by saying I appreciate you all being here today! As you know, the Humane Society is something I've been involved with since I was in elementary school and it deeply warms my heart to see people turn out to support such a fantastic cause. I also want to say a special thank you to my good friend Eliza Wood who helped coordinate this event, and to the lovely staff at Cyc who've pitched in to make it a success. Enough about that, let's go kick ass for dogs! And cats!"

"Dogs? I'm about to die for a bunch of fucking dogs," he snipped under his breath as he limped into the discotheque studio. He made a b-line for her but the third wheels beat him, and he ended up two rows back in direct view of Jared. The divine's sense of humor continued to be unrelenting. Five minutes in, he wanted to murder Jared and the third wheels, but not before setting fire to their matching neon leggings and the red accented machines on which they rode. Ten minutes in, he was one pedal away from dying on his red accented machine.

Jared then singled him out:

"Theo, I see you there my friend! You look like you had a good night last night. I've seen you in the gym, you're not this out of shape."

"God fucking dammit Jared," he wheezed. This sequence continued for the remaining 35 minutes, though he didn't hear Jared's persistent barbs again until the final five, at which point he felt tremendous, amazed by his ability to spin through a hangover that would've killed the most weathered sailor.

"Nice of you to join us Theo." The room laughed. Eliza turned towards him.

"I never left."

"I see that." He then acknowledged the room. "Now I pick on Theo, but I know he's not the only one who suffered through today. You all have, and I want you to use this cooldown to celebrate what you've accomplished. Whatever happens the rest of today can fuck off. We did it for the dogs! And Cats! Gotta give love to the cats!"

The class ended and he approached Eliza who was now speaking to Jared:

"Hello friends."

"Hi! How are you? I'm glad you could make it!"

"I wouldn't have missed it. Sorry for the sweat."

"Oh, don't worry about that. Have you seen me?" He had, and the sweat only made her Catwoman suit more seductive.

"True, but I still feel gross."

Jared then interjected. "We're going to Forage. You want to join?"

"Absolutely. I'm ravenous."

"So you did have a good night?"

"You could say that." The trio then frolicked, or so it seemed, through the early spring wind, arriving a few minutes later barely able to contain their hunger. After sliding into the narrow wood and slate booth and consuming their first savory bites, Jared inquired:

"Did you both enjoy the workout?"

"I did! Although I forgot how hard your classes were."

"Theo?"

"In a demented way, I did. By far the best hangover cure I've ever encountered."

"Would you mind putting that in writing?"

"For a round, sure."

"Deal. Eliza, I haven't seen you in forever. How's everything?"

"Getting better. Long ways to go but it's less chaotic."

"What have you been doing?"

"Until recently, nothing besides working out and watching movies with my parents. This week I dove into some school work which was refreshing, and not as maddening as I remember."

"Does this mean I can expect to see you at Double U this fall?"

"I hope so." The pair kept talking for what seemed like an eternity, no pause long enough for him to interject. He boiled with rage, fed up with his invisibility. Jared did eventually open the floor, albeit with the most unfavorable subject:

"You're awfully quiet Theo. Last night catching up with you?"

"No. I'm always quiet."

"True, but you're abnormally quiet. What gives?"

"Nothing. I'm fine."

"Sure you are."

His tone turned brusque. "Really Jared, I'm fine. Can we talk about something else?"

"Not until you tell me what lead you to zombie through my class. I've seen people with one leg move faster."

"I had too much bourbon."

"What kind?"

"Does it fucking matter? I showed up, didn't I?"

"Whatever you say my friend." He leered at him, her speaking before anything further could be said:

"I should be going. It was great seeing you both! Thank you again for coming!" As she walked out a torrent of fury engulfed him. It was the first time he'd seen her in four months and thanks to Jared's inquisitiveness, he now looked like an angry drunk. He snapped:

"You just had to know what the fuck happened last night didn't you?"

"Whoa, whoa, whoa. Why are you getting all hot and bothered?"

"I haven't seen her in four months Jared, that's the only fucking thing that got me out of bed this morning, not the fucking dogs, oh, and cats. All day I've been blocked, diverted, drowned out, and I'm fucking sick of it. And then, when I finally did get my chance, it was to address irrelevant bullshit about why I was hungover, which is none of your fucking business, especially because I've seen you far worse, on a Tuesday afternoon! That's what's got me hot and bothered." He took a deep breath and scanned the interior for onlookers before continuing. "Look, if you must know, we had a pregame at my apartment and I was hooking up with a girl when she texted me. As soon as I saw her messages I ended it. And believe me, with this girl, that was no easy task." He took another breath as he lowered back into the booth. "There. You happy?"

"I think you need to take whatever you got going on and redirect it. You showed up looking like death, not me. Another word of advice, stop clinging to her."

"I'm not clinging to her."

"You are, everybody and their grandmother can see it."

"I'm not fucking clinging to her!"

"Your actions say otherwise."

They parted ways. He was at the end of his tether, no fuses left to short, transferring his torrential anger onto others, his own worst enemy, a familiar narrative playing amongst different scenery. Only one path would resurrect him – finishing the novel.

XIX

Through faded lenses he scanned Forage's contemporary dark interior in the wake of yet another social blunder. Wherever he went, however hard he fought, the scared boy still governed him. He walked home mentally and physically numb. Thankfully, the apartment was empty, enabling him to peacefully remove his repulsive clothes reeking of sweat and ethanol without facing a trial. Following a warm shower and changing into nondescript grey sweats, he left to write, deciding to do so at one of campus' most isolated locations – the stacks at Memorial Library.

The stacks were a claustrophobic labyrinth of 1970's beige vinyl flooring and old books with individual cubicles lining the south wall. It was the opposite of College Library: no cafés, rowdy Greeks, or views of Lake Mendota to be found. What it did have was seclusion, exactly what the day required. Two Ultra Monsters, one red, one blue in hand, he entered the dungeon.

He pounded the keys with rooted tenacity aimed at him, intending to vanquish him completely before exiting. He didn't know what he was writing, only that the page count was increasing, leaving him pummeled with each uptick. Five hours later, he stopped, exhausted by the inhumane effort, in awe of the page count, 257, and the last sentence:

The scared boy now vanquished.

Those five words crystallized the true intent of his prophetic work. It wasn't to create an alternative universe or to tell his story, it was to annihilate the squatter who'd puppeteered him the last ten years.

It was the boy, not society, not the patriarch, not his community who'd led him astray.

His first step outside was a baptism, the spring air the holy water. He looked toward the end of State St. and saw *Wisconsin's* glow once again piercing the night sky. "No," he thought, "too soon. You can't go back, not until he's gone." Frank then swooned in with the interlude to My Way. He filled his ears the rest of the night, the only interruption caused by the vibrations of his electric toothbrush, the soft piano keys finishing In the Wee Small Hours of the Morning as he laid a navy blanket across his chest.

At the store the next day, he was able to churn out another 30 pages, bringing the novel's total to 287. His goal was to have a 300-page manuscript before editing, a feat he would achieve later that week on Wednesday night. The last sentence was written behind the store's counter at 6:53PM, seven minutes before closing.

The trilogy was set...

He gathered his things and headed to Riley's, the iconic liquor store three blocks west. Fresh 101 was the only appropriate libation for such an achievement.

Following another successful deception, he slipped the libation into his backpack next to the vending machines outside the entrance. With every step, he felt the glass shifting, clinking, each subtle movement an indicator he was incrementally closer to breaking its red seal and displacing the contents into a deserving ice-filled vessel, the best reward for completing this stage of his arduous undertaking.

From the safety of his room, he removed the 101's paper coat and admired its hourglass figure. He spun it clockwise and counterclockwise, sensing its every nuance starting with the matte label donning the "101", discerning where the paper ended and the glass began, grazing the stamped lettering below its neck. Though he'd drank many bottles before, there had never been such theater surrounding one's consumption. Commemoration was in order. He grabbed a felt pen from his desk to inscribe the label – *March 18, 2015, First Draft Done*. As he began to write, the undisturbed crimson stain, appeared in his periphery. A gentle sigh refocused him from the grim symbol of sacrifice.

Exiting to the living room, the anticipation continued to grow. The ice-filled vessel had been meticulously prepared, ready to receive it's caramel partner. A forceful twist broke the seal with a satisfying tear before being accompanied by an equally satisfying whoosh as the cork and glass separated. The theater concluded with the asynchronous cracking of ice. The first sip spread through his mouth like fire through an iron basin on a warm summer night. "That's the stuff," he whispered to the empty room.

Shortly after preparing the Peasant Spread, he positioned himself in the middle of the couch closest to the kitchen. He did not intend to leave that position except to refill the vessel. A communal joint would've been nice, but he valued solitude more in this moment of celebration. Sitting back with a finished plate and fresh glass, he turned on the TV expecting to see Bea, Betty, Estelle, and Rue conversing on the veranda. However, the picture featured a crotchety old man, a pair of squabbling psychiatrists, and the old man's British caregiver. It resembled a show Kristoff introduced to him while out at their Christmas lunch.

He watched the disjointed quartet with keen eyes, their dynamics equally if not more entertaining than those of the four hags he'd grown to adore. It was the humor and the backdrop on which it was painted that captivated him – a graceful fluctuation between sharp wit and slapstick comedy set amongst a quirky metropolis. His affinity for it grew by the minute, longing to reside in such an elegant post-modern apartment resembling the house of the matriarch's parents in Northern California. Nostalgia inserted itself alongside the 101, and the trio set off into a world they all could inhabit.

XX

The next morning began with addressing the mild effects of last night's libations sitting half empty on the miniature refrigerator adjacent to the bedroom door. Luckily, Derrick had left more stagnant coffee than usual. Its guzzling provided a comforting sense of routine necessary to begin another stale day of conversing, folding, and sorting.

The front door opened to a frosty lake breeze. It wasn't the icy hurricane he'd grown accustomed to during February, and for that alone he was grateful, its subtle chill now comforting his aching forehead. Summer Wind's soft saxophone interlude began populating his ears, affording credence to the auspicious start. These notes and more of Frank's ballads further reinforced the mellow ambiance as he strolled down Langdon St.'s slight decline onto the 500 Block of State St. He entered the store to Steve standing erect in front of the register intently watching the news.

Ex-LSU Quarterback Sentenced to 15 Years in Prison

The staunch headline populated the banner at the bottom of the screen. "They got him, hugh?"

"They did. Unbelievable." Steve's depressed tone struck him as odd. "You haven't heard from Eliza, have you?"

"I saw her last weekend."

"When you see her again, tell her I'm glad this ordeal is behind her."

"I will."

At 11:00AM, he received a message:

Hey, what are you up to tonight?

It was the alignment he'd yearned for, yet skepticism pulsated through his head like a sprinting heart. He'd committed to resting for the next two days before starting the editing phase, days which currently consisted of nothing except bickering psychiatrists and the remaining 101. Anything with her certainly eclipsed both the former and latter, and he responded to her message with great enthusiasm:

Nothing at the moment. What did you have in mind?

Double U? Maybe with Jared, Jessica, and Jocelyn?

The alignment sharpened further, baring a cryptic resemblance to four months ago, ensuing unease as he aimlessly wandered around the back half of the store. Both of their lives were now dramatically different; he an emerging, spiteful writer on schedule to complete his first novel and her an intelligent, recovering idealist whose path remained uncertain. There was no doubt this Thursday night in March would differ from its predecessor.

I can get behind that! What time were you thinking?

8:30, before all the cabanas get full, you know how it is when it gets above 40.

Do I ever. See you tonight.

6:47PM. The ambivalence brought on by this meeting had at least made the day seem short, as it did with the walk home in the chilled spring air and preparation of the Peasant Spread. The 101 in his room called shortly the spread had been devoured. He answered, placing it on the coffee table before preparing its vessel. No sooner did the first sips of charred caramel flow down his throat was another helping required. Another sip, then the angst surrounding his upcoming encounter roared back, pinning him to the suede whilst his overactive psyche pinballed. "Quit being a pussy." A gulp, then out the door he went.

The last time he'd made this trek the air was cold, the atmosphere heavy, and his only focus impossible inebriation. The temperature alone was a reminder of how distant he was from that time, his careful intentions and enhanced taste for alcohol providing further credence. 7:47PM, his favorite aircraft, and the bouncer was returning Hank's I.D. "Jameson rocks, please."

Double U did not supply 101. In fact, at the moment it didn't supply much of anything. A group of backwards-hat, polo-donning frat boys were playing darts in the corner to the right of the staircase, a stack of four empty pitchers situated on the high behind them. They were the only action at the moment. He walked upstairs to find two groups of girls stationed at the cabanas spread around the perimeter dressed in variations of textured jackets, tight pants, and western fray boots. It was 40 degrees, after all. A sunburst sky marked by purple and slate claws oversaw him as he took his place at the third cabana. If nothing else, he was appreciative to be a lonely fleck against this canvas.

After much rumination, Eliza, Jared, and the other two finally appeared. Against the backdrop of faux cowboys, her green down coat, mid-rise dark wash jeans, and wolf grey turtleneck was a welcomed site, along with her ever alluring walnut curls, a shade for which the world's finest whiskey's could only pray. The other two blended in with the existing vanity seekers.

"How about this," he contently opened.

"How about it," she replied, gently caressing him, "I'm glad to see you."

"The feeling is mutual." For a brief instant, the other three vanished along with the canvas as their eyes locked in a lustful standoff. "Jared, Jessica, Jocelyn, how are y'all doing?"

"My novelist friend," Jared exclaimed, "you're looking much better than the last time I saw you!"

"Wasn't my best was it." Humility would be the tone for the opening rounds. "What do y'all want? First round is on me."

"Nonsense," she proclaimed, "tonight everything is on me. You have all been incredibly supportive over the last few months. It's the least I can do. We'll be right back."

The surroundings blurred again as they casually strolled to the bar, the crowd no larger than when he arrived.

"What are you having?"

"Jameson rocks."

"Two of those, and three vodka sodas."

"Whiskey? When did this happen?"

"My dad and I have been watching a lot of Clint Eastwood and John Wayne movies. It's the only appropriate drink."

"You don't say? I began drinking it when I decided to become the next Hemingway. I like your story better."

"I like your circumstances better."

"Touché. In all seriousness, how are you?"

"I'm good. Ready to come back. I'm going to take some classes over the summer so when I start in the fall I'm not too far behind."

"That'll be good for you. I'm sure sitting at home is starting to get annoying."

"It served its purpose."

"To your comeback."

"I never left," she glowed.

They sat on opposite sides of the cabana with Jared on the end and Jessica and Jocelyn against the railing. The words transversing the table were of no significance to him, all he did was focus on her, a fun game to play with copious amounts of whiskey. An equally fun game was watching her glass and guess when she'd take her next sips, which were closer to gulps. If only Clint and John could witness such beautiful savagery.

"I'm ready for another," he stated.

"Me too," Jared interrupted.

"Shall we Eliza," he signaled towards the bar.

"We shall."

"I'm glad you texted me earlier. Your timing was perfect."

"How so?"

"I finished my novel last night."

"That's fantastic! How'd it turn out?"

"I'll let you know in a few days."

"Well until then, we'll assume it's For Whom the Bell Tolls." They raised their refreshed glasses. He appreciated the continuation of the Hemingway analogy, and further appreciated the possibility his fury over the last four months could've resulted in a masterpiece. If nothing else, he improved his ability to drink middle-shelf alcohol and proved he could write 300 pages of prose. Maybe he was closer to Ernest than he thought?

"Three tequila shots please."

"What are you doing?"

"Jared, get over here. I have a present for you." He hustled from the cabana to receive the gift. "I finished my novel last night, all 300 pages of it, and whether or not it's 300 pages of literary perfection or 300 pages of diabolical shit is irrelevant. What is relevant is we are standing on the spot, well, a level above the spot, where I told you two I'd do it, and much like that moment four months ago, I don't care about what transpires tomorrow; I care about what transpires tonight. I sincerely thank you both. I know I've often made it difficult for you. God help us all."

"God help us all," they replied in unison.

"In all seriousness, thank you both for not judging me."

"Once again my friend, you've managed to surprise us. I didn't think you had the courage."

"I did." She seductively gazed at him.

"I'll leave you two alone." He suddenly felt a gentle graze on his right arm, then a silky set of fingers interlocking with his. He turned his head to find her sultry expression staring into his soul:

"Let's go someplace quiet." The incredible nature of the unfolding scene mirrored that of him and Elena's. The parity shook him, and he began to violently rub the fingers of his free hand like mating crickets, the burn of which validated his consciousness. They descended the staircase without acknowledging each other, their woven fingers the only point of connection. "No, not there." Arriving outside, they turned due west towards Lake Mendota. Soon, they were at the stairs of Memorial Union, but they didn't stop to admire its ivory majesty. They passed Science Hall, then entered the Lakeshore Path.

"Where are we going," he asked.

"Someplace quiet, trust me." The walk dragged on, but soon, a clearing emerged. On the left was a two-story concrete monolith, a pair of shut garage doors on the first level. On the right were two docks. He knew where they were – Porter Boathouse, only a half mile from his dorm. She let go of his hand, "look familiar?"

"Very." They sat down on the incline leading to the docks. "Why'd you bring me here?"

"Isn't this where you and Elena go?"

"Elena?"

"Yes, from your story. The girl who's supposed to be me." He now remembered sharing the latest copy with her in a fit of rage following his terse encounter with Jared last Saturday. A battery of perplexing emotions flooded every orifice in his body, freezing every appendage except his head baring a humiliated expression. "It was the Edgewater dock. You actually read it?"

"I had a lot of time on my hands, and I wanted to see what led you to quit school. I understand now."

"How much did you read?"

"All of it."

"You read 257 pages in five days?"

"Like I said, I had a lot of time on my hands."

"I wish I hadn't sent it then. I was in a terrible mood that day. It was probably 257 pages of diabolical shit." His humiliation quickly degraded to depression.

"I'm glad you did. Is it a masterpiece? No. Do you have some work to do? Yes. But, I felt your heart in every word, and because of that, I fell in love with it. You're a special person, Theo, and special people don't come into your life often. When they do, you need to show them how special they are." She continued to lean in closer, her J'Adore filling his nose. The air between then vanished as their passion unfolded under the moonlight.

Their bodies intertwined and slowly lowered to the frigid concrete. The fictional reality articulated only in his writing was now manifesting gloriously. They briefly separated, allowing the J'Adore to be replaced by the soft northwesterly breeze rustling the leaves of the overhanging trees. One fell to the ground inches away, causing them to separate again. He held it in his fingers and felt its ribbing. The irritation in his skin was the only validation he needed to continue embracing.

"What are we doing," she laughed.

"What do you mean?"

"This is crazy. We're friends."

"What's wrong with that?"

"Friends don't hook up on docks."

"What if we're more than friends? Is that so hard to believe? You said it yourself; special people don't come around often, and when they do you need to ensure you show them how you feel. You're pretty damn special yourself, Eliza."

"Thank you, but I still don't feel comfortable with this. I didn't mean to lead you on. I think I should go." She slowly unraveled.

"Wait." He exhaled, firmly grabbing her left arm. "Can I walk you to the Union?"

"Sure." That affirmation would be the last word spoken that night. He led her to a yellow Crown Victoria at the base of the Union's steps, waving goodbye as the door shut. He stood in disbelief as the car disappeared past Science Hall, acutely aware of the parity between his prose and his reality. Each woman left him in a cavern of impenetrable darkness, uncertain if he'd witness light again.

XXI

He navigated towards *Wisconsin* as only a steadfast Shackleton disciple could. The anticipation of her right arm was the only entity upholding his sanity. He passed the drunks on State St. with contempt, his head perpetually swiveling. With each step passages of his novel played and replayed, their words screaming above the drunk's zealous dialogue. The cacophony was then interrupted by the site of the fountain's worn brass top and unvandalized concrete arc.

He leaned against it exhausted, his breath heavy with Jameson. Looking up, his muse welcomed him, arm pointed due south. His body relaxed, exposing the tension in the back of his legs and the tender blisters now inhabiting his heels. Painful as these sensations were, he was elated he could feel them. Now sitting at the fountain's base, he began admiring her golden figure and the noble white behemoth supporting it. The pair instilled a tear in his right eye, reminding him of the journey he'd undertaken and the irrevocable pain it'd inflicted.

"Forward," he uttered her symbolism under his breath. "Forward. Forward...that's it! That's it!" The sudden epiphany brought the scene into sharp focus, his left index finger and arm were now in an unstoppable gyration. "I knew it! I knew it would come to me! Thank you!" He stood up, the imprint of the arc pulsating through his already stiff posterior. The painful sensations continued up Wisconsin Ave. and worsened as he turned onto Langdon St., where art-deco monolith of the Old Edgewater then appeared.

The hotel was a relic from the patriarch's time at Wisconsin. It was the political elite's lounge of choice, the lakefront bar providing the perfect setting for a night of hush dealmaking and private inebriation. Jutting twenty five yards past the bar's entrance was the dock on which he and Elena embraced. It's two legs were barren this time of year; in the novel they were lined with white hulled speedboats. Soon, he found himself amongst the interior's Cherry and Walnut cladding, a fresh golden totem in front of him. "You mind if I take this outside? It's a pleasant night, albeit a little chilly."

"Of course, sir." The bartender replied.

The soft northwesterly breeze that graced him only a couple miles away now blustered in a torrent of anger. He attempted to drink the totem but his action was swiftly refused by the angry winds. The dock creaked and surged over the violent surf to such an extent he couldn't envision him and Elena at its end. He returned inside and took his place amongst the room of muted suits and accompanying Old Fashioneds.

He could hear their conversations with greater clarity than those of the State St. drunks. To his left was a politician and his wife speaking to a pair of lobbyists about a proposed traffic circle. Behind was a gay couple attempting to articulate the drama of a friend named Jessica. This particular exchange intrigued him. He swiveled around to the unmistakable flamboyant tone of Jared's voice, then quickly swiveled back. He then heard footsteps patter next to him:

"Excuse me, can I get two more Martinis? Dirty with two olives, please...Don't be coy Theo, I see you there."

"I could say the same thing. Why aren't you at Double U?"

"It got too crazy, so I met up with Aaron."

"Who's Aaron?"

"A lawyer I'm trying to hook up with."

"Well don't let me disturb you."

"Actually, I'm trying to buy time. His wife may show up."

"What the fuck?" He was once again questioning reality. "What? Why are you getting two Martinis then?"

"For him and his wife dipshit."

"Ah. Excuse me, club soda and lime please. Go take care of business then come sit here."

"Will do my friend, thank you." Jared quickly took care of business, handing the cheating bastard his Martinis before taking his seat at the bar and sipping his virgin cocktail. The bastard's wife arrived shortly thereafter. They both felt sorry for her, for what a tragic moment it would be when she discovered the truth. "She's got no idea."

She then appeared at the end of the bar next to them. He only managed a brief glance before returning his focus to the half-empty totem, though he didn't need much more than that to observe the dichotomy between her gilded appearance and raw alcoholism. "Barkeep, who ordered these drinks for me and my husband?"

"I believe it was your husband ma'am. He's sitting over there."

"I know where the fuck he's sitting. What I need to know is why somebody who hates olives would order two dirty..."

"...Actually, dear, I've grown to appreciate them lately. Now, let's sit down." The bastard guided his intoxicated spouse behind them. Jared's eyes were fixated on his glass, the encounter clearly terrifying him. He shifted in his chair, attempting to flee before being barricaded by his leg.

"Relax. You'll reveal yourself if you leave now."

"I'm using the bathroom, but thanks for reminding me."

Just then, the floor clinked with the sound of block heels, followed by the rasp of an aging cougar. "Excuse me, did you by chance see who ordered these Martinis for me and my husband?"

"I did not, ma'am."

"Well somebody ordered them!" She was now performing to a growing crowd of attentive guests. "And I need to know who the fuck did! I know this scum fuck has been cheating on me with one of you, and when I find out who, the two of you going to wish you never fucking left that shag shack where you've been hiding! Now I know it wasn't this nice queer sitting at the bar, that'd be too easy. Maybe it was the queer sitting next to him? Maybe..." Before another vulgarity could be mustered, her husband smothered her out the door and onto the patio, followed closely by two hulking security guards. The bartender dialed 9-1-1 as Jared reentered the picture, his face appalled by the wrestling exhibition now taking place through the glass and the rabid screaming directed at him from the bastard's wife.

"Fucking cunt," the bartender remarked as two officers arrived to remove them.

Jared returned to his barstool. "Something strong that isn't a Martini, please." The bartender and guests laughed at his wit. Somehow, even in the most compromised position, he managed to elicit positive reactions from complete strangers. It was this charisma which made him a force at the front of spin class or any crowd, a trait drawing his ire since the day they met. "Thank you," he said as the bartender handed him a tall Gin and Tonic.

"That was something."

"You have no idea."

"Tell me, what happened at Double U that made you come here?"

"You really want to know?" The Gin and Tonic was now a mountain of ice.

"I do."

"Aaron is Jessica's older brother."

"And I take it she found out about the two of you tonight?"

"Yes. She found out everything. You could see the lightbulbs in her head going off like a Christmas show. I thought I was going blind." He couldn't help but smile at the imagery.

"I shouldn't laugh. How'd your relationship with him start?"

"Jessica invited him out a few weeks ago. We hit it off, then after she left we had some tequila and he began revealing some things, then after more tequila he revealed everything. After that night he started coming to my Tuesday night spin class and we began meeting for dinner twice a week on Capitol Square. It was then Jessica began telling me her sister-in-law was becoming suspicious. No patent attorney has multiple client dinners a week on Capitol Square, neither does a student. She thought he was cheating on her, and that somehow I was involved. I came up with every excuse in the book, even that I was seeing a state senator, but I couldn't keep her at bay any longer. She snatched my phone at Double U while I was texting him." He chuckled. "I think she finally put two and two together when she saw 'Aaron Sneaky Lawyer' as the recipient."

"Wow." He was without words for the first time this evening. They downed their respective elixirs as they debated the implications of who would speak next and with what tone. "I'll have another."

"Me too." The bartender acknowledged their requests with great enthusiasm for he wanted the story to continue. Seconds later, their next round was in front of them.

"What are you going to do now?"

"Stop messing around with married men."

"And?"

"And what?"

"You did just confess to sneaking around with one of your roommate's married brothers. Don't you think you need to mend that relationship before embarking on another conquest?" There was no humor left in his voice, and little left of his second totem.

"Since when do you care about my personal life?"

"Since we became friends."

"And when was that?"

"I don't know Jared. Call it the second week of British History. Call it the third. Call it never. I don't give a shit. All I know is I'd be an awful person if I let you walk out of here without a plan to fix this situation."

"It's not your situation to fix. It happened. It's over. Life goes on. Stay out of my personal life." The sentiment behind his words mirrored Eliza's the night of his seizure. Rather than quivering with a soft affirmation, however, he downed his totem, slipping his last $20 on the bar as he marched away.

"You know I'm right."

XXII

The remark he made minutes ago stuck, its verbiage identical to that the patriarch would've used. Although he claimed otherwise, he could no longer deny their striking similarities.

However unlikely their friendship, Jared now laid claim to a fractal in his life. Above everything else, he despised watching gifted people ruin themselves, and Jared was one of the most gifted he'd met.

*

The prodigal son from Burlingame, CA, he grew up in the stereotypical Silicon Valley household consisting of two parents with long careers in tech and who bought real estate at the right time. Money was never an issue, but plenty of other areas balanced it out, among the most egregious his untimely arrival.

They never made plans to have a child, and even after his birth there was little emotional investment to ensure a loving home, although their financial investments could bring a small country out of debt. Among these investments was attendance at the elite Crystal Springs Uplands School. He flourished, fueled by a burning desire to obtain the attention of the aloof breadwinners. Every activity and club in which he could partake he did, excelling at them all, though his real passion was film and theater. His bedroom was lined with prints of his favorites –Book of Mormon, Fargo, Pulp Fiction, Fear and Loathing in Las Vegas, Wicked, and

Natural Born Killers. They covered the full comedic spectrum – cheerful and light to dark and psychedelic – mirroring his reality.

One night his junior year, the aloof breadwinners revealed their true selves in unspeakable fashion.

Following an evening of cruising, drinking, and smoking with his fellow thespians, he stumbled through the front door to a dimly lit living room with a deep house soundtrack attempting to hide the bodies of six adults taking turns between partners, sex not a factor. The breadwinners never saw him. He'd had his own suspicions about his sexuality, but witnessing his parents and their socialite friends freely engaging in such experimentation affirmed his homosexuality.

A year later he conveyed his desire to attend Wisconsin for its excellent communications program. From that perspective, it wasn't a lie, but his real desire lay in its distant proximity and surety he wouldn't see anybody from Crystal Springs. They agreed, and come August 25, 2013, he left, never to return to Burlingame.

*

"I wonder if his film is prophetic as well. That would've made for one hell of a scene. Maybe if he asks I'll remember it for him." He annotated the events in his phone before entering the apartment. Derrick, Hank, and Kai laid under a light fog, eyes fixated on another creation from The Book of Mormon playwrights. Jared would've appreciated the site. All three turned to greet him with muted nods. "Stoners, save some for tomorrow, I've had enough action for a while." More muted nods.

The night's libations made navigating his bedtime routine eventful. Trying to sleep in this state was pointless, so he rejoined the stoners in hope the fog would serenade him to sleep. He woke at 3:48AM to a head heavy with libation side effects and legs heavy with those of exercise, both preferable to the spins. The stoners were gone, their remnants sprinkled over the coffee table. He briefly considered compiling the remnants for himself before dragging his numb body to bed.

A lighter weight welcomed him in the morning along with a gentle cool breeze trickling through the window. Seeking an auspicious start, he rolled onto the floor and began his recently developed habit of performing 100 pushups immediately upon waking. When the cycle of work and writing started, he had little energy left for any further exertion. A few weeks ago, his body reminded him of such neglect, and he began exercising intensely on a regular basis, though still not a frequently as he'd prefer. The consistency of his push-ups gave him solace his physical health wouldn't degrade to that of other areas in his life.

The usual Stop and Shop combination uplifted him as he opened the store and waited for Steve and Kelsey to arrive. An hour later they were still absent. Another hour, still no sign of them. Finally, at 11:45AM Steve walked in with a bandaged face and bloodied knuckles, followed shortly by Kelsey in a pair of black sunglasses and messy bun. "You two had eventful nights."

"You have no idea," Steve replied.

"Did you get into it with the plumber?"

"Hard to say, just remember he was a big motherfucker who wanted a piece of Kelsey."

"You two went out together last night?"

"Yes. Kelsey told me she's going back to school yesterday. We celebrated at Double U."

"Interesting. Who's going to be taking over for you?" He saw the opportunity to take advantage of their hungover weakness. Classic Machiavelli.

"Don't know yet."

"Any reason I couldn't?"

Steve then interjected. "None that I can think of, but don't take that as a yes. We'll talk about it on Monday."

"Fair enough." He walked smugly back to his post. It was a quiet day, affording ample opportunity to ponder his standing with Eliza and Jared. He held both in high regard. He admired her uncanny ability to oscillate between a shrewd, Rockefellian operator and warm, maternal sage. Equally, he admired his magnetic rhetorical skills and unapologetic self-confidence. As he went about the store's upkeep, the events of last night circulated, his angst growing stronger with each round.

The store's delirious operators left in silence just before 5:00PM, further concentrating the angst. The temptation to reconnect and explain himself was strong, but the necessity to edit a 300-page manuscript was stronger. He couldn't afford any distractions while

Pandora's box remained. It'd be best to silo last night for the time being.

Leaving the store, a beacon of light streamed from the North, the only enlightening element in an otherwise noir scene. Recently, Frank had been accompanied by his fellow Ratpack member Dean Martin along with the stylings of Bobby Darin. In a most appropriate fashion, the soundtrack to this remedial walk home started with Everybody Loves Somebody, followed by It Ain't Necessarily So. The divine's humor never ceased to amaze.

The soundtrack concluded with Dean melodizing "Per chi pal-pita d'amo-re". Hank and Kai were seated in the same position as they were during last night's fog, equipped with the ingredients for another round. "May I join?"

"You can," Hank responded, "but you need to supply the wine."

"The wine?"

"Yes, we're out. I'm thinking a nice Malbec. What about you, Kai?"

"Yes. I love a good Malbec."

"Go on." He shooed him away.

"What the fuck's a Malbec," he thought as he reentered the noir with Bobby and Dean. Asking for help at University Liquor was out of the question; it was the one rule you couldn't violate if you were underage. To his benefit, the drabby shop only had one option, and $10 later he was carrying its flimsy brown sleeve into the darkening cityscape, craving the earthy smoke and the accompanying ascension.

Passing the bend of University Ave. onto Gorham St., he encountered a group of girls sitting on the Chaser's patio donning light grey sweatpants and matching Wisconsin crewnecks. One stood out with her peach birthday sash and matching crown, a nice complement to the establishment's signature Jumbo Strawberry Margarita. It was a sight he'd scoffed at many times, only in this instance the sash was adjacent to an enchanting cascade of brown curls and burgundy lips supporting a pair of bright sapphires whose ancillary gaze bored into his soul. He waved, hoping the creature would recognize him. She retorted with cruel disgust.

"Hey, are you at Chaser's?"

"No. Why do you ask?"

"No reason." Those two words were all that filtered through his puzzlement.

Frank began carrying him home with a gentle reminder. "And then I go and spoil it all by saying something stupid like I love, you." He couldn't fathom the girl's resemblance as the darkness peaked his senses. His cadence intensified with the crinkling of the Malbec's sleeve now increasingly audible inside his coat, his eyes darting in every direction seeking further abnormalities. Finally, he arrived home, no ghosts in sight. Never had minor law bending and mistaken identity adorned anyone with such paranoia.

"What'd you get?" Hank inquired.

"It was the only one they had." His hand twitched like a Parkinson's patient.

"Whoa!"

"I know, not the best but..."

"...No, your hand. What the hell happened?"

"Can I sit down?"

"Yes, of course." He took his place among the suede's comforting grime.

"I went to University Liquor. Everything's normal. On my walk home I see this girl at Chaser's in a light grey sweatsuit and peach sash who looked identical to Eliza. Terrifyingly identical. I waved to her and she looked at me like I was a pedophile. I called her, and she told me she wasn't there. Ever since I've been paranoid."

"So you saw the ghost of Eliza?" Kai entered the conversation and began layering in the fog.

"I suppose."

"Sounds like a case of stress-induced psychosis. You need to get back to writing, you're mind's acting up."

"What's stress-induced psychosis?"

"It's a phenomenon I read about in my MCAT prep book. Basically, you begin to hallucinate after prolonged periods of sleep deprivation and stress."

"Interesting. The doctor believes stress was the primary cause of my seizure. It makes sense. I'll start editing tomorrow, hopefully that'll help. May I?" He took the bowl from Kai. The events of last night certainly would've explained the latter cause, but he wasn't willing to elaborate. He watched as the green and hazel flakes tangoed with the embers before removing his thumb from the side hole, allowing the apartment air to force the viscous smoke into his expanded chest. It then exited, carrying with it a school of pins that cut into his throat before the severity forced him into a coughing fit.

"Easy Tiger." The fit continued, each cough lifting him into the next atmosphere. The ascension, despite its ferocity, was familiar. Unfamiliar was the dull buzz vibrating through the rest of his body only allowing him to pass the bowl before anchoring him to the suede.

"What is that?"

"A spliff. Half tobacco, half weed."

"I'm not sure how I feel about it."

"Try some Malbec." He slowly sipped the jam-like liquid, also unfamiliar. He enjoyed it, it's smoky tannin profile pairing well with the scars of the burnt leaves. Until now he'd only had wine from a glass bottle at Christmas, every other time it'd come from plastic. "What do you think?"

"Beats the bag." The other two chuckled.

"It's not bad actually," Hank, the resident sommelier, stated with pleasant surprise.

His Malbec would sit there for some time. The ascension and buzz continued to accelerate, quickly becoming intolerable. There were no stimulating thoughts, just overwhelming sickness resembling that of copious whiskey, only now he couldn't stand up to relieve himself. The only option was to hold on.

Soon, the experience calmed and the sickness subsided. He noticed the empty bowl on the table with three half-full glasses alongside the open Malbec, the cork barbarically shoved in the bottle. The other two were fixated on the animated obscenities spewing from the television. He no longer cared for this scene. Still unsteady, he tip-toed to his room and closed the door before lowering to a comforting location at the edge of his bed.

This scene was all-too familiar, and although the torrential physical sensations subsided, the void quickly filled with equally torrential psychological ones. Perhaps it was the parity with what he'd experienced in this spot at the beginning of this journey? What laid in front tomorrow was more unchartered territory he'd need to navigate alone. The mystery of those 300 pages tore at him until the ceiling disappeared.

XXIII

A slate hue cast over his room signaled the arrival of the new day, though it felt much closer to a new era. Today was the day Pandora's box would reveal if he'd spent the last four months sculpting a geometric gnome or the Venus Di Milo. The smoke scarred his throat, forcing him to keep his mouth shut until liquid sustenance could be found. Trudging through the living room he saw the coffee table scattered with ash and raw tobacco, a memorial to last night's turbulent flight. He scowled at the remnants while healing the scars.

As to where he'd spend the rest of this momentous day, that would be the lake view desks at College Library, where he deemed the work of the previous summer disgraceful and began anew. There would be no whiskey this time, merely enough coffee to give an elephant violent tremors. He filled a pint glass with ice and poured over the cold remains of the pot Derrick left for him.

Derrick hadn't been in the picture for some time as he'd taken a job at Babcock Dairy requiring him to leave before dawn. He missed him. It was their fraternal banter which gave him an idea of what it'd mean to have an older brother, a gaping void he'd become increasingly conscious of this past year. As with the events of Thursday, however, this sentiment would need to be siloed. Finishing the last of the pint, he returned to his room and prepared for the day. He left at 7:30AM, an hour earlier than that of a normal work day. Instigated by the hatred towards the cracks in his personal life, he aimed to finish editing the entire manuscript that day. Whether or not the task was realistic was irrelevant. When fueled by spite, no target was too ambitious.

Neither Bobby, Dean, nor Frank joined him on the mile walk to the library. For once, he desired the natural ambiance provided by an apocalyptic Langdon St.. Devoid of any sentient beings, he could hear the young leaves bristling in the light wind blowing from the west, the lively birds layering in an emphatic tenor. The duality induced an optimistic outlook, which when contrasted with the decaying 20th Century Greek behemoths encouraged his amateur philosopher side. "Nature has given us a damn near perfect canvas to begin our work, and yet we chose to build street after street of eyesores. Fucking Christ. Nobody will be sad to see them go."

Architectural pessimism aside, he was now in the shadow of his arena. The front desk attendant greeted him with apathy, annoyed by his early arrival. Her sentiments were easy to ignore, and now with a desolated library to himself, he strode up to the coveted window desks, warmly greeting them like a platoon member.

He eased into reading his work. Word after word the pages went. Some stretches induced great pride. Others caused him to question his sobriety. So far, however, he was satisfied with the outcome, though even the most perfect sections required minor adjustments. One hour in, he'd covered 25 pages, rewarding himself with a weak Americano from the downstairs café. It didn't take long upon his return to lose himself in the work. His stochastic review evolved into a fluid evaluation interrupted only by grammatical or thematic dams quickly disposed of through violent typing.

The library's population increased considerably as the clock struck 11:00AM. He finally looked up after desperate pleas from his aching neck, though he immediately regretted it:

"Hello Ernest. Hard at work I see."

"That I am. What brings you here?"

"Finance 300."

"Sounds like hell."

"Hell's got nothing on this nonsense."

"That bad huh?"

"Yes. The only positive is it keeps my mind off more difficult things."

"I know what you mean. Would one of those things be a certain romantic coup that occurred on a dock two nights ago?"

"Maybe. Difficult is a subjective term. You of all people should understand that."

"You think I would." He noticed she'd now deliberately organized her side of the table. "Would you want to grab lunch in a couple hours? I feel I owe you."

"Why do you always say that? You don't owe me anything. Quit acting like a pedantic step parent." He didn't respond. The flow that carried him the past few hours disappeared. The pages lay stagnant, their once harmonic melody now a matrix of meaningless dribble. Most of his energy was now dedicated to avoiding contact with a dissipating dream. He began to wish last night wasn't a case of mistaken identity. Another seizure would've also been welcomed.

"I'm taking a break. Are you going to be here a while?"

"Yes. Where are you going?"

"Don't know. Just not here."

"Don't be too long." Him and his stoic glare marched towards the stairwell now lit by the midday sun. Outside, Madison appeared as if it emerged at the Empyrean. "Where has this scene been?" The worn limestone of Memorial Union and the contrasting rust of Science Hall shone alongside the sliver of emerald emerging from the base of Bascon Hill. As he continued east, the emerald sliver grew larger and was further complemented by the light sapphire of a freshly defrosted Lake Mendota.

He arrived at Union Terrace and sat down on top of the stairs adjacent to the docks. His mozzarella and tomato bagel provision was consumed quickly; apparently his flow had made him ravenous. A steady tide crashed and receded from the lower steps. Every few crashes, freshly thawed drops of melt would escape and wet his hands, already clammy from the steady southern wind traversing the shoreline. It wasn't the most comfortable place, but it provided the peace and separation necessary to continue the day's expedition.

Her recent remark sat at the forefront of his increasingly fragile psyche. She'd exposed him yet again, only this time he'd managed to escape without a gurney. Though her step parent analogy didn't cut like the psychoanalysis in her apartment, it still managed to induce deep melancholy. He stared into the waves hoping answers lied beneath the choppy wash. Eternities passed as he travelled in and out of the depths before a mechanical whoosh drew his attention skyward. The sound lead to a single white and navy-bellied airliner crossing at cruising altitude. He followed the flight path with eager eyes as it vanished into the horizon along with its turbine soundtrack. It wasn't much, but it left behind a wash of clarifying sentiment that calmed his turbulent mind.

She was right. He was pedantic, he was too dependent on others, and he wasn't who he should be, to no fault but his own. A heavy truth, it was. As rapid as its onset, however, it subsided even faster, and he now stared at the sky and navy horizon floating higher than any green flakes could take him. It was the enlightenment he'd been searching for; the key to shattering the interlocking chains preventing him from acting on the underlying spirit of the golden sage garnishing the Capitol. He rose from the steps free.

"The summer wind, came blowing in, from across the sea...It lingered there, to touch your hair, and walk with me..."

He played the verse on repeat enroute back to his post. She hadn't moved, paralyzed by her numerical inferno:

"Welcome back."

"Thank you," giving her a warm smile, to which she replied with a wary leer.

"What are you so happy about?"

"I had a nice break."

"It sure looks like you did." He said nothing, maintaining the same warmth as he sat down and reestablished his flow. When his neck cried out again, he was at page 140, the new halfway point in his much improved work. He noticed her zipped backpack was the only entity across from him. As the searing pain in his rhomboids spread through his body, he elected to mirror the backpack's state and end the tumultuous day on a high note. He sat and awaited her return. "You look like shit."

"I feel like it too. I didn't realize the toll editing 140 pages takes."

"Apparently it's quite a large one."

"Indeed. Show a fledgling writer to the door?"

"I think that can be arranged." They left, exchanging meaningless logistical pleasantries as they exited into the vibrant cityscape. Though there was still a clear barrier bisecting them and her tone remained frosty as the melt, surface level interaction was no longer an obstacle. Soon, they passed the steps of Science Hall, to anybody else forgettable, to him it was haunted by Elena's ghost, the eeriness fortified by the presence of her inspiration in lockstep next to him.

With the steps out of view, he calmed. They continued their stroll through Library Mall and appreciated its restored fountain along with the lush grass that surrounded it. They then found themselves in the shadow of St. Paul's. At the beginning of last year, he frequented the church every Friday for noon mass. This routine was short-lived, and by winter it'd ceased, only returning once for Easter that spring. The dispassion he felt towards it and the congregations occupying it momentarily receded as he pondered the coincidental sequence of the week's events through the fragile lens of divine intervention.

They arrived at the parking garage at the intersection of Lake and State St.:

"Care for a lift?"

"To where?"

"Someplace quiet."

"I think that can be arranged."

XXIV

"Alright, where are we going?"

"Nothing's coming to mind. Every place I know on campus is either closed or noisy."

"So let's go off campus."

"How about James Madison Park? It's just past The Edgewater."

"Wonderful." She zipped her red Fiesta towards the exit. Turning right onto Lake St. with equal quickness, she then raced the tiny hatchback through the Greek houses. "Such a waste of architecture on such bratty fucks, still can't believe you were almost part of one."

"Well, technically I am part of one."

"What does that mean?"

"It means I'm a member of one through the end of the year."

*

His membership amongst the Greeks was a closely guarded secret. His parents forbade him to join his freshman year, arguing he should be concerned with academics instead of eponymous fraternizing. Their point was valid, but like many of their instructions he ignored it out of spite. He joined the patriarch's house and was initiated in the fall.

Her disdain originated from a party she attended during her senior year of high school at a neighboring house, Alpha Beta Sigma, the largest on campus at the time. Tyler's friend Neil was newly initiated and invited them to a party during the spring. At the party, he was treated like a king as a touted recruit. To the contrary, she received a near lethal dose of cheap vodka and Rohypnol. They were separated the entire night, only by coincidence meeting at midnight, enabling them to exit just in time for her to exhaust enough vomit to clear her system and avoid a hospital trip. Her hangover lasted several days.

The next morning, the two of them recapped the night's events in an intense debate in which he claimed she cheated with several of the brothers, including Neil. She clung to her innocence, not of inebriation, but of loyalty. Later that week, they discovered the truth as Neil revealed several brothers were discovered sneaking date rape drugs to the girls. Her story was corroborated, though the resentment between them was not eased. It was a story they'd take to their graves.

He first heard this account when they started working together at the store. It came up organically, and ironically, just before he planned to ask her to his Spring Formal. Needless to say, her story crushed that dream. As his feelings for her deepened beyond lust, he did reveal he pledged the fraternity, but never disclosed his membership. His challenges sophomore year would've lead to him leave regardless, his history with it dying with the spring bloom.

Why he revealed it now is a mystery left to the heavens.

*

She continued her race past the Edgewater and soon arrived at James Madison Park. "When were you planning on telling me this minute detail Ernest?'

"Never. I'm quitting this year. If it's any consolation, I haven't told parents. They still don't know, and never will."

Her face expressed many emotions, none of them favorable. "I really should make you walk home right now."

"I get it..." he conceded, his hands gesturing in defense.

"...But I won't. I'm just going to ask you this: what else?"

"What else?"

"What else are you hiding?"

"Nothing. You know how I feel about you, you know how I feel about my life, and you now know I'm a soon to be ex-frat boy. There's nothing else." Her displeasure softened, although it still paretoed disgust. She turned away and stared at the water. After several seconds, she exited the car and began pacing towards the lakeshore. He let her walk, thinking it'd be wise to give her space and that she wouldn't go far, but she didn't stop, quickly moving east along the path. He jumped out and gave chase. A few dozen yards into his run, he saw her collapse onto the concrete path.

He arrived seconds later to the site of raw fetal sobbing. He crouched down, gently rubbing his hand on her back. "It's okay." She looked up, her eyes bloodshot with tributaries of tears streaming down her rosy cheeks. After a momentary stare, she lunged forward and tightly wrapped her arms around him:

"I'm sorry," she wept, "I don't know what I'm doing. I've been deathly afraid since that day. I never leave the house. Not because I don't want to, but because if I do, I'm afraid the moment I'm alone somebody will attack me. I've tried to take baby steps to get out more but it's been fucking hard. And it feels like every time I do, something happens which makes me regret doing so."

He continued comforting her in silence until her weeps turned into sniffling breaths. "I'm here, and I'm not going anywhere." He then eased her off the ground and escorted her towards the car. They passed a bench and sat down, him still comforting her in his arms. "Look at the lake. Isn't it gorgeous?"

"It is." She managed to crack a slight smile.

"Can I ask you something?"

"Yes."

"What's the best thing I can do for you right now?"

"Don't leave." She burrowed deeper into his chest. There they sat admiring the light chop as it hit the breakwall, the splatter barely eclipsing the corrugated rust, the mid-afternoon sun beaming down on their chilled bodies. The wind gusts were now light breaths delicately contacting their skin from the west to east, offsetting the searing of their sun-kissed faces. It was a scene his dreams hadn't yet painted.

"What should we do now?"

"I think I've taken up enough of your time. Why don't I take you home?"

"If that's what you want." The rationality of his responses hid profound disappointment. Progress never seemed to compound, and it was increasingly isolated to his unfinished work. He was beginning to empathize with the many artists who went insane on their mission to reach immortality. He carried his work with him in every picturesque view of Madison, in every touch he shared with her, in every sip of intoxicating fluid flowing down his throat. Even as they walked to her car amongst the serenity of the luscious greenery and pale blue water, a piece of him remained stationed in the novel's verbose labyrinth.

They remained silent until arriving at his apartment. He looked at her hopeful his discrete sorrow would beam through and this would not be the end of their day. The apathy in her face suggested these signals were ineffective. A hollow "I'll see you around" punctuated their intense encounter.

Inside, he welcomed the site of a still apartment populated only by the ash and dirty glass layered on the coffee table. After jettisoning his public appearance, he made his way to the kitchen counter armed with the fixings of a Peasant Highball – a house pour of 101, $0.69 grocery store seltzer, and a lemon wedge cut with a dull, rusted butterknife. It came to be after reading an article about Hemingway's favorite cocktails, all of which were complicated mixological potions except for the Highball, which only required two cheap ingredients any starving artist could afford. The name "Starving Artist Highball" nauseated him, so he settled on the bourgeois "Peasant Highball" variation.

Libation concocted, him and the Highball took solace amongst the complementary filth. The refreshing first sip temporarily lightened the fog following the first day of editing. He turned on the TV to the NCAA Basketball Tournament which began two days earlier. A close battle between Ohio State and Arizona played in the background as the mess of ash and glass in front of him became intriguing. Perhaps the Highball needed a friend? He began checking the vessels for remnants. Inside the stainless steel cylinder used to grind the leaves, he found just enough to compose a hit. He placed the scraps into the bowl and set them ablaze. The charring he'd experienced his first few hits had softened to a warm breeze that tenderly brushed his esophagus. For better or worse, he'd adjusted, the rocketing takeoff now a gentle glide.

Another Highball sip allowed him to melt into the filth with ease. He sat contently numb, the greatest sensation in his unexplored world, praying Ernest and his grandfather were watching over him with empathy.

XXV

The apartment remained still well into the night. A few more Highballs and hits managed to sneak their way in and now it was time to retire for another long day of editing. As he closed his door, he heard the apartment unlock, followed by a loud slam and a series of lead-footed stumbles. "Fuck me man, god damn it, why the fuck...AHHHH." The cacophony was unmistakably Brody. He wasn't around much, though the last couple week's he'd made a point to venture a weekend binge. Lord knows what he'd gotten into tonight. The last sound was a faint clap as he'd presumably located his bedroom.

7:08AM. His body ached from the excess of the past few nights. It was a reminder this level of degeneration wasn't sustainable despite the novelist label. After putting on a pair of navy sweat pants and a Wisconsin hockey jersey, he waddled into the living room to find Brody curled like a fetus on the far couch in a wrinkled white button down, navy chinos, and chestnut oxfords. As he walked through the kitchen the fetus creaked and moaned, shifting to the mirrored fetal position. He poured him a pint glass of ice water and accompanied him on the opposite couch. More creaking and moaning ensued, this time resulting in him seating himself upright. "Fuck me man."

"Rough night?"

"Something like that. God my head hurts. Is this mine?" He pointed to the water.

"Yes sir."

"Thanks man." He gulped down the pint. "One second." Brody strode to the bathroom, instantly slamming the door and hoarsely heaving every molecule from his insides. He knew the feeling all too well. If college had taught him one thing, it was he was a puker, and not a quiet one. Brody returned a couple minutes later:

"I've heard quieter exorcisms."

"Me too," he chuckled. "That was something."

"So how'd you end up like this?"

"Our startup idea didn't make it to the next round. Such bullshit, but it's whatever. It probably wouldn't have won anyway. My group went out afterwards, and halfway through Veronica called me, which she said she was going to do, but I didn't expect it that late or to be that drunk. I don't know what I said but I pissed her off so I just kept drinking and somehow made my way back here."

"Sorry to hear that. At least it's over."

"True. It's been a rough year."

"I think everybody in this apartment has been through some hell this year. Makes you wonder who stepped on the burial ground? Or who left their drink unfinished?"

"True. Everybody goes through stuff though. It enables us to grow."

"It helps when you have a group of people to share it with too. I never had that until I moved in here. I don't think I could've made it this far without you guys, even though we haven't interacted much lately." They acknowledged each other with a single appreciative nod.

"By the way, how's your book coming?"

"Well, I managed to get through the first half without scrapping it, which was a major victory. We'll see how today goes."

"When are you trying to publish it?"

"End of summer, before the next semester starts."

"Do you think that's realistic?"

"As of now I do. Then again, I also thought my work from last summer was a masterpiece. It's hard to be definitive in unchartered territory."

"I know what you mean." Brody was raspy, his disappointment beginning to show. "I thought we had a real game-changing idea this year, until the competition committee tore it apart. It doesn't matter how good you think your idea is, until it's outside your echo chamber it's impossible to validate it. And even when it's validated, it's still a crapshoot if it makes it to the level you envisioned. I say all that to warn you: be ready to fail." He was surprised by this counsel, particularly from somebody with such eternal optimism.

"I'll keep that in mind. I really should get going." Since December, he'd successfully repressed these saplings of doubt by denying all thought ancillary to work and writing. As he gathered his things for the second day of editing though, they emerged, and within the first few steps outside, they blossomed. Not even Frank's best could suppress the circling vultures inside and out. On Langdon St. he passed two rotting racoon carcasses: one fresh with blood in the middle of the street, the other mummified bone and pelt pressed against the opposite curb. Above them, the slate skies blanketed the emerging spring. Auspicious, the start to this day was not.

He finally entered Memorial Union and purchased a large coffee from the shop inside the east wing. Placing it on the table next to the bay windows of Lakeview Lounge, he removed the lid and allowed it to cool. After setting up the rest of his space, he took the first sip, the burn of which caused him to throw 24 ounces of molten dark roast onto his laptop. The machine went black as he frantically flipped it into an upside down vee on the adjacent chair while hoarding fistfuls of napkins from the neighboring tables. The spillage was swiftly contained, although dire consequences now faced him as the comatose machine was the only place he kept the novel. He allowed a few minutes to pass before attempting to bring it back to life. It failed, and would for another dozen attempts.

No computer stores on campus were open Sunday. The only option for remedy was 20 minutes away at West Towne Mall, which he wouldn't be able to get to for another seven hours due to the weekend bus schedule. The seeds of doubt were now in full bloom as an eternal wait faced him. Thus far, Brody's ominous warning had manifested. He stared into the noir lakefront like a cynical longshoreman, flustered by the sudden turn.

Just then, an elderly man in a fraying grey cardigan and wrinkled khakis entered the Lounge walking slowly in his direction. They noticed each other, though he was in no mood for visitors. He returned to the bleak landscape:

"May I sit with you young man?"

"Um, sure."

"Thank you. You looked lonely. I thought you could use some company, especially since your computer appears to be out of commission."

"You're right about the latter."

"You know they don't like coffee very much." The elderly man acknowledged the dark brown outlines surrounding the device. "Beer they seem to be fine with though."

"Do you know that from experience?"

"Well I can't speak for these new slim things, but the old units we used could tolerate a good beer, maybe two."

"I seriously doubt that." His elbows were now on the table, his face being upheld by firmly folded hands hiding a fugasi smile.

"I supposed you'd have to been there. Tell me young man, what's important on that device?"

"What difference does it make?"

"None. I was a psychiatrist for many years. I got to know all kinds of people. Some I wish I didn't know so much about, some I wish I knew more. Identifying symptoms came easy to me. Within seconds I could diagnose everything from Munchausen Syndrome to Narcissism to Transference. It quickly became boring, so I began probing for deeper, more subjective reasons behind my patient's diagnosis: things like what did he or she value, what interested him or her, what did he or she want for their future, and so on. And you know what I discovered?"

"No."

"I found those qualitative factors ultimately determined whether my patient got better or worse. Medication can fix a lot of things, but it can't fix a person's soul, nor can it force a person to let go." He was now intrigued by the rambling shrink and allowed himself to ease into the chair, crossing his arms in a congenial manner.

"I've never heard that perspective before."

"It's an original one. I even wrote a book about it."

"What's it called?"

"Yesterday is Gone. You won't find it anywhere though. I never published it."

"Why not? It sounds like a great story."

"I didn't publish it out of respect for my wife Elizabeth. I came up with the idea while she was going through terminal breast cancer. It was her way of reminding us to live in the present and not long for the days when we were able bodied. It kept us sane. After she passed I made a promise to write that story in the most eloquent and precise way I could as a tribute to her, and to not publish it, as desperately as I wanted to. Elizabeth was quite private and would've abhorred the idea of her story being shared with the world. It took me ten years to complete."

"When did you finish?"

"Yesterday. This is my first trip to downtown since I started writing it." He was astonished by the shrink's dedication, and more astonished by the coincidence of his appearance. He continued to sip his coffee in peace while he fumbled for a response:

"I suppose if I were to tell you my sulking was due to my book potentially being lost over a broken laptop, you'd think pretty low of me."

"I believe you think low of you, but I don't have enough evidence to definitively state that. Tell me more about your book." He then proceeded to unveil the novel's every detail from the arc to the challenges in writing it to the characters he substituted for real figures. It was the first time he'd described the story in this depth, an especially draining exercise given his current state. Yet after he finished articulating the last summarizing words, a vivaciousness began flowing through him. The shrink was quick to notate this drastic shift. "I'm happy you've found a pursuit that excites you this much. It's rarer than you might think."

"It's exhausting though."

"As is every great endeavor on which mankind has embarked. Don't fear effort. Fear the outcome of not having to impart any."

"Yes sir. I feel I owe you something. Probably a lot given you're a psychiatrist."

"Well as I said, I was a psychiatrist. Now I'm just a man, an elderly man. I would love to read your book after you've crafted it to your standard."

"I appreciate that. Where should I send it?"

"Just bring it here on a Sunday morning. I can promise you I'll be here from now on at this exact time. You know how reliable an elderly man's routine is."

"That I do." The gardening and walking rituals of his grandfather came to mind. "To whom should I address it?"

"I'll tell you that when we meet again."

"Okay."

"It's been a pleasure young man. I look forward to our next encounter." They exchanged a warm handshake before the shrink exited to the opposite end.

*

Over the summer, he visited the Lounge every Sunday morning to verify the persistence of the shrink's routine. As promised, the routine was steadfast, sitting at the exact spot they had their remarkable encounter.

On Sunday August 23, 2015, he arrived at the Lounge just after 8:00AM holding a copy of his completed work – Forward, A Madison Story – in one hand, and 24 ounce dark roast in the other, top firmly secured. In his left pocket was a black felt-tip marker he'd been carrying the last week whilst delivering copies to his Madison community. The Lounge was empty. He sat at the same table, now identifiable via a faint water stain in front of the west-facing aisle seat. He waited all morning for the shrink, but he never came.

Confused, he left the lounge, suspecting he'd chosen the one week he'd broken routine. However, he returned the next Sunday to the same sight. Fearing the worst, he searched the State Journal obituaries page:

Dr. Hugh Robert Williams, August 21, 1925 – August 22, 2015

His eyes became flushed as he stared at the eerie void across from him. He gently put away his computer and centered the book in front of him. After wiping his eyes with the bottom of his shirt, he autographed the reserved copy:

Dr. Williams, or Hugh, not sure which you'd prefer,

I just missed you. Hopefully you and Elizabeth will find time to enjoy this work. As promised, it is to my standard. I hope it is to yours also, and is a proper tribute to the wisdom you imparted on me that fateful Sunday morning in March. I look forward to our next encounter.

Thank You,

Theo

XXVI

The Sunday ended with his computer functional and him still in awe of the shrink. Ten years to perfect his story; how that time had withered him. He could only speculate how often he grew bored or got lost during those years. He knew he would've.

Ten years was half a lifetime ago. At the start of it, he was a bright eyed boy who yearned to imagine and eventually manifest those imaginations into tangible entities – a beautifully simple existence. The passing years, like the shrink, had left him scarred. Gusts from every direction blew and battered him, no beacon in sight. Somehow, he managed to navigate to calmer waters, a distant flicker now over the horizon. He readied for the final effort that'd return him to that existence.

BAAAP BAAAP BAAAP

A daisy and ash piano colored the wall on his right, the contrast piercing his cracked eyelids and rendering the green digits on his bedside clock illegible. The shrink had gifted a newfound determination to finish, and finish well, well above his highest expectations. He swiveled into an upright posture at bed's edge before methodically preparing for the day.

In this season time had no meaning. Any ancillary task to editing and working at the store was neglected with the exception of the daily exercise bout. The only interaction with the roommates was just before bed, never more than five minutes. He kept his parents abreast of his activities every few days, also for never more than five minutes. The same was true for Eliza, Jared, and Steve, who still didn't know the reason for his availability was due to him writing a novel. It was a lonely time.

April 24,2015. A frosty burst from the unseasonable cold billowed into his room, the goosebumps tingling his uncovered torso. Too alert to continue his slumber, he went about his morning ritual with the monotonous precision of a sentient droid, departing an hour earlier than usual. The exhaustion from the past month of scrupulous editing had calloused him beyond imagination. "This is a testament to the human spirit," he thought as he took his first few steps across the house's weathered porch. Outside the gate, he stopped, pivoted to the east, then strode towards the intersection of Langdon and N. Carroll St.. He owed an old friend a visit.

She anxiously awaited his arrival, requesting a blue opening from those above to accentuate her shimmering figure to aid in his navigation. He arrived as the last flecks of the flaming canvas gave way to their muted azure and pewter counterparts, seating himself on the weathered concrete arc chilled by the glacial front.

Gazing up, the crippling exhaustion soon evaporated as the sun rose higher, replaced by serenity, serenity in knowing the next few days of rest were well earned. His confidence of a path to the end was now unwavering. Another two weeks of final tweaks, then it'd be ready for critique by his selected confidants.

The muted scenery was scheduled to be illuminated in all its spring glory tomorrow, allowing him to reconnect with two of said trusted confidants for a day of restorative debauchery. He initiated the outreach after tidying the first survey of misplaced clothing:

I hope you're both well! I know I've been absent for some time. Tomorrow is supposed to be beautiful, and I would love to celebrate it with you two, assuming you'd be willing and able? Say noon at DLUX?

The day inched by with dead silence. He knew they had good reason to alienate him, though he remained optimistic after the day's supreme beginning. 7:00PM arrived, the invitation lying dormant. The night brought moderate inebriation courtesy of the last drops of 101, but no replies, the befuddling latency bringing into question their prestigious label. "Fuck them," the words slipped through as he was cocooned by the linen bedsheets.

Their inactivity continued into the morning. He hit the floor as he'd done every day for the last 60. His arms pumped wrathfully, hands digging into the carpet, strangling its threads with the ferocity of a famished lion. Each pump pressurized his torso linearly until it could no longer hold the ballast of hot blood. Normally, this is when the pumping stopped while the pressure released around 50 repetitions. The sinister emotions towards them, however, pushed him past this mark, climbing to 60, 70, then halfway through 81 his bulging triceps gave way, his trunk hitting the floor like an axed spruce. He repeated the cycle three more times for a total of 137.

After seizing his arms during the final repetition his torso collapsed again from a greater height than the previous three rounds, his calcified chest cushioning the blow. He rolled onto his back and gazed at the matte beige ceiling, heavy breaths rapidly pulsating his ribs. This moment had become his favorite part of the day. The thoughts in his head, like his fatigued muscles, ceased to move, and he was able to bask in the stillness. Normally a couple minutes, today it seemed infinite. The moment did eventually end, leaving a crisp spring day to be enjoyed in unrestricted solitude. First, a trip to Fresh Market at the corner of University Ave. and Lake St. to replenish rations barren since Wednesday.

The blossoming trees appeared outside the front door and were soon joined by the compilations of Bobby, Dean, and Frank. He traversed the vibrant streets of post-hibernation locals and suspiciously happy shame walkers with cartoonish optimism, and carried it into the market as he plucked his essentials from the glossy shelves. He finally turned off the soundtrack to unpack onto the clerk's conveyor belt. While making small talk, an unmistakable black outline came into his periphery. Like a siren to a weary sailor, his vision darted, and behold was his elusive confidant, painted with a freshly saturated Catwoman suit, hair bundled in a straight low pony darkened by the same perspiration. With a meticulously packed load in each hand, he cautiously approached from the right. She turned in his direction, acknowledging his presence with a curious smirk:

"Well hello."

"Hello indeed. How are things?"

"Good. And you?"

"Also good." The interaction was extremely awkward, like strangers incidentally touching hands while reaching for the same pepper. "Anything special planned for today?"

"Not really. I just finished my first spin class as an instructor."

"Oh really? And how'd it go?"

"Really well, but I had a good assistant."

"Jared?"

"Yes. He was supposed to meet me here."

"I have to ask, did you see my message?"

"I did."

"Are you interested or no?"

She exhaled a shallow breath. "No. I'm not."

"No problem. Maybe some other time."

"That'd be nice." He exited, depleted by the harsh rejection confirming his alienation hypothesis. The burn induced by the weight of the groceries climbed up his forearms, reaching his biceps as he crossed University Ave. and turned right past Double U. By the time he crossed State St., his arms had inflamed beyond their state earlier that morning. The sear fueled him, and he arrived at his apartment vindicated by the aggressive effort. The debauchery could now begin. But first, the Peasant Spread, which had been recently modified to include rice instead of the bourgeois pasta and was now topped by a sprinkle of jejune low fat mozzarella.

Spread empty, he moved to select his attire. A glorious day demanded class. He'd developed an affinity for sharp dress shirts earlier in the year when his prospects were brighter. He owned two, both shark collar, the first solid powder blue, the second China blue with white vertical stripes and a white collar. He chose the latter then complemented it with tapered ash chinos, a cognac leather belt, distressed tan penny loafers and maroon dress socks, garnishing the ensemble with matte black aviators. He rolled the shirt cuffs twice-over before coyly exiting his room. Derrick stood in the kitchen. "Somebody's looking to do some damage."

"Indeed," he swiftly replied, opening the front door to a muted overcast empowered by flowering vernal shades. Turning left, he headed to the initiation point – The Statehouse restaurant inside the New Edgewater Hotel.

The heavy steel handles teleported him. Arcs of glimmering brass shone on the floor against sliced and polished granite cliffs of every color, leading him to the coveted bar whose warming cedar woodwork welcomed him into the bygone era. He took his place amongst the gild and mulled over the cocktail menu. He needed a new tonic, 101 had grown old. "What can I get for you, sir" said the bartender adorning a classic black vest and tie over a white French collar rolled to mid-forearm.

"I'll have an Aviation." Gin seemed like a natural progression.

"Excellent choice."

He gleaned over his destination as the bartender prepared his drink whilst making small talk with the gentleman at the opposite end. The frothy lavender elixir soon arrived. After a brief examination, he grabbed the stem of the champagne coupe, the black cherry hitting his upper lip as the first drops entered. "Quite alright," he muttered while holding the coupe halfcocked above the bar top. The second drops came shortly after.

Setting the coupe down slowly, he examined the gentleman more closely. He looked familiar upon second glance, though from what he could not remember. Another sip soon clarified his resemblance to the sneaky lawyer, who judging by the daintiness with which he held his handful of whisky had been there a while. Flicking the last sips into his wobbling head, he rose, siphoning a $100 bill on the bar before striding toward the entrance. He pincered the coupe's stem with his eyes fixated on the cocktail menu, hoping the resemblance wasn't mutual. He passed behind, then paused in the entryway before turning judiciously in his direction.

XXVII

The sneaky lawyer stumbled away. His pulsating heart calmed. "How's the Aviation?"

"Very good. I'm going to need at least one more." Another sip. "I'm going to move outside."

"Go right ahead, sir."

He passed through the dining room endowed by more gild, the mahogany tables bracketed by teal felt chairs organized on an ornate ruby carpet with pine accents giving way to an empty patio fenced in by varnished wrought iron. He took his seat in the far right corner, recuperating from the near calamity brought on by nobody other than the comedic divine, whose humor would soon reappear.

He reentered for another Aviation. A few more souls now populated the bar, their spring attire reminiscent of polo players and their female spectators. None bared any familiarity though, a welcomed relief as he returned to the empty patio. The sky remained hidden behind a flowing grey and white canvas, the lake a deep and still aqua interrupted by a handful of small white cats crossing at speed from west to east. The sight was a pleasant one, preferable to the forecasted picturesque spring day.

This stage of the journey was near the end. Only a handful of unscrutinized pages remained before he'd step aside and allow those he trusted to guide the novel to its final destination. The trouble was, he didn't know who these trusted individuals were.

Eliza and Jared knew him and his story the best and would take his "be as brutally honest as possible" directive seriously. However, they were more distant now than ever. Aside from them, there were his roommates, none of whom would have the insight nor the time required. There were his parents, who he feared alienating. The sentiment behind his writing was honest, though many anecdotes, particularly those of shameless inebriation, would horrify them. He was also concerned it would lead the reader to abhor and question their competency as parents. That would be the greatest injustice. They'd adorned him with boundless love and set the best possible example. He chose to veer astray.

He watched the grey snakes slither leisurely above the water as the second Aviation disappeared. The final lavender sliver consumed, he set down the coupe to a most unbecoming site – Eliza and another man on the opposite end of the patio sitting close, stamped copper in hand. To the divine comics he again turned, "really fuckers?" Their table was enroute to the bar, the only salvation in an otherwise nightmarish reality. "Well if you insist," he uttered to the comics.

"Theo?" He sighed in defeat before rapidly turning coy.

"Eliza? What are you doing here?"

"Same thing as you – drinking."

"I see that."

"Come join us! This is Neil. Neil, this is Theo." He knew the name and the history with it all too well.

"Pleasure to meet you Theo." A towering Irish masterpiece with bleached wavy hair, he wore a white oxford button down, slightly wrinkled, cuffs rolled just above the wrist with royal blue chinos, hems rolled just so his ivory ankles would showcase his chocolate bits. He accessorized the ensemble with tortoise Steve McQueen Persols and a steel Aquaracer with a deep blue dial. Jared's dream.

"You as well Neil. I'm going to grab another drink."

"Sounds good. The Normandy Mule is excellent."

"Duly noted." He sped through the dining room to meet the lonely bartender. "Hello again."

"Hello sir. What will it be this time?"

"Stella please." The bartender twirled a glass from the rack above and orchestrated the proper ritual, ending with an emphatic skim before passing him the chalice. "Thank you, sir."

He returned to the table and sat on her left opposite the masterpiece. "Stella, excellent choice," he remarked.

"One of Belgium's great contributions to the world, along with Spa and Jean Claude, obviously."

"Indeed!" The masterpiece laughed. "I remember going to the brewery in Leuven when I was abroad in the fall..." He continued, but his story soon became white noise. The eyes beneath his inferior Ray Bans fixated on her, scoffing as she leaned into every word of his adventures: Oktoberfest in Munich, bicycling while stoned in Amsterdam, clubbing in the ruins of Budapest, yachting on Lake Como. Somehow, he'd made all of these activities unappealing.

"Wow, sounds like you had quite a time over there," she finally interjected.

"It was incredible. Such an eye-opening experience." Their drinks had been empty since Munich. "Looks like you guys could use another round, as could I. Same thing?"

"Yes," they replied in unison. The masterpiece swiftly departed.

"So, what do you think of him?" She asked.

"He's something."

"And that something would be..."

"...Pretentiously evangelical."

"I thought they were good stories."

"Oh please. I've heard those stories a thousand times. He just frolicked through a compilation of Europe's most stereotypical travel experiences. The only eye-opening thing he did was take the wrong pill."

"Somebody's a little jealous."

"I'm not jealous. I just can't stand when people claim to have done something eye-opening when all they've done is do what everybody else does. Do something that's actually different, or at least don't talk about the same phony shit as everybody else."

"Alright. What would you talk about?"

"Little things. Things without vanity, such as pulling over in a roadside bar enroute from Stuttgart to Trier and watching the US-Germany World Cup match with a German family, the dad of which had a Dallas Cowboys star tattooed on his right shoulder.

Like eating beef tartare in the bowels of a 15th Century restaurant on the shores of the Rhine in the shadows of the 800 year-old gothic masterpiece known as Cologne Cathedral. Or falling asleep in the backyard of a friend's house in Lommel on a red sun chair while two brown cows grazed in the neighboring farm. That's what I'd talk about."

She'd now leaned into his words the way she'd done with the masterpiece. Normally an unhinged ramble would've discomforted the other, though it appeared to have done the opposite. There was no time to theorize why for the masterpiece returned carrying his Stella in one hand and their mules in the other. "Carrying two mules like that was a struggle. I don't know how the beer maids did it."

"Very carefully," he sarcastically retorted, raising his eyebrows in her direction. She angrily returned the gesture.

"You know, Neil, Theo is working on publishing a novel."

"Is that so? What's it about?"

"Well," he began the summary with hesitation. He'd never been showcased like this before, and the aftermath of the last rant in her presence landed him on a gurney, a fact which suddenly manifested in his throat like a nest of spiders escaping a flame. He continued, praying the scenery would remain. "It's about a college sophomore who's fed up with trying to conform and quits to write a book. In the process of doing so, he's forced to deal with the consequences of going against convention, what it means to deeply pursue an interest, and," he paused, "how in the end it was a worthwhile journey, one to which he'd dedicate his remaining years." The masterpiece leaned back in his chair, sipping his mule before bringing his right hand back to his face, his index finger covering his typically lively lips. She too was bewildered by the concise summary. He reached for the Stella knowing his work was something of indisputable substance, and that it wouldn't be his last.

XXVIII

The table's silence endured long enough for the first ray to fracture the dreary canvas.

"Wow," the masterpiece finally spoke, "how long have you been working on it?"

"Since November."

"And when are you going to publish it?"

"Mid-August. I've been editing it for over a month now and I'm fixing to send it to people for feedback."

"I hope it works out for you." They toasted, the clinks bringing with them a significantly more gregarious tone. They continued trading stories at The Statehouse for another hour before leaving for Double U. He and the masterpiece were getting along favorably, though both were in obvious competition for her affection. She was sandwiched in the middle on the half mile walk, the masterpiece maintaining a subtle lead position. They emerged from the neighboring alley to a line of drunks 100 yards long. Navigating their way to the front, the masterpiece began a brotherly negotiation with the bouncer, concluding with a stiff handshake masking five folded $20s. They entered the madhouse.

The madhouse was filled with a spectrum of preppy spring tones regurgitated from a Ralph Lauren catalog. Their outfits were outliers, in particular her white lace Victorian blouse with sandstone pants and penny loafers. They felt superior as the masterpiece forced his way to a pocket at the bar's far edge. "Three Gin Rickey's please."

"What's that?"

"Gin, club soda, and lime." The bartender turned away.

"Guy doesn't know what a Gin Rickey is, can you believe it?" Actually yes, he could, because he didn't know either.

"What's a Gin Rickey," she whispered.

"Don't know. Something he had whilst attending a garden party in Kensington with the Duchess of York, probably." She smirked as they were handed the Rickeys. The trio then proceeded upstairs, arriving at the patio amongst another catalog page, the models packed like sardines. A pocket emerged near the railing on the street side. "I'll have that." He forged a path through the models. "Cheers to the madhouse," he toasted, the other two replying in unison from opposite sides. "What a day, eh?" Neither of them replied to the additional commentary:

"Theo, there's something I should've told you."

"What is it?"

"Neil and I are dating." He glanced at the masterpiece, now baring a sheepish grin.

"I see. I should've figured when I saw you together at The Statehouse you weren't there as friends." His head sank disheartened into his exposed chest garnished by formulating beads of sweat. "I'll leave you two alone. Thanks for the hospitality,

Neil." They shook hands. "See you around Eliza." He vanished into the models, looking over his shoulder to find the neighboring cabana was the one from last month. The comics didn't earn a response this time.

"I told you inviting him would be a mistake."

"I don't think it was. You two seemed to have a good time. And look, now we're alone."

"You shouldn't have toyed with him like that."

"You could've spoken up."

"And said what? Sorry guy, we're on a date, bugger off?"

"Oh stop saying bugger! You aren't in fucking Kensington!"

"And you aren't thinking straight!" The sudden explosion rapidly sullied the mood. "This was a mistake." Droplets of sorrow freckled with black slowly emerged from beneath her rose gold Clubmasters.

"I couldn't have said it better myself. Goodbye Neil." She sliced worked through the polo crowd. Emerging on the other side, she hurled her drink into the trash bin, the glass clamoring through the pit of crushed aluminum. She made her way down the stairs and out into the daylight. Like many nights prior, she kept her emotions at bay until to the Lake St. corner.

In front of him was a half-eaten roast beef and provolone on wheat surrounded by ejected shredded lettuce and giardiniera, the preferred sustenance whilst gawking at passing drunks through the shop's window. He was wounded, the outcome now chiseled in stone. She and the masterpiece, though he was a pompous cliché, shared a tightly braided history. He also appeared to be from incredible means, able to provide for her in impossible ways, however he came into them irrelevant. Impossible was also the apt description of his long attempted conquest the masterpiece swiftly ended. In many ways, he was grateful for his pompousness for it made her the villain, dulling her seizure-inducing psychoanalysis and disqualifying every judgement she'd imparted.

Outside, the stream of drunks was interrupted by a white lace and sandstone streak slithering upstream. It was an unmistakable site, though it no longer induced anything but apathy. Just another drunk.

He left the shop and walked towards the Capitol with fresh blisters rubbing the inside of his loafers, prompting a detour back to the apartment. He took the opportunity to remove the preppy garb and replace it with his preferred attire: red Wisconsin hoody, denim blue t-shirt, black joggers, and a pair of worn white and royal blue Nike tennis shoes, accessorized with a used two-tone Tissot passed down from the patriarch. The vast majority of his writing took place in variations of this outfit along with the vast majority of his working days. It was as soothing as the white terrycloth blanket he had as a boy. Upon tying the Nikes the pain from the blisters disappeared and he continued his easterly trek.

The green of James Madison Park was awash with dogs and humans of all ages enjoying the final hours of sunlight. Their distant, joyful discord combined with the occasional yelp from the circling seagulls scored the scene beautifully, gently reminding him of his true desires. Associating with the likes of the masterpiece and his fellow pompous Greeks – dressing piously, drinking for vanity, prowling for French kisses and blow jobs – wasn't remotely desirable. It provided nothing. He much preferred the scene unfolding in front of him – serene, unobstructed by manufactured happiness.

He found the vacant bench where him and Eliza sat a week earlier. He took his place on the emerald metal, his breath slowing as the plank's subtle chill entered his torso and upper legs, his arms propped on the top plank, right leg crossed over left. The heavy chop splashed against the breakwall as the forceful wind rattled his ears. He aimlessly scanned the horizon, watching as the seagulls were rapidly swooped into the darkening navy sky. No pinballing thoughts, no leaps into the future, no retracing of the past. All of him was there.

Then, the metal below him vibrated: his phone adorned by a familiar name.

XXIX

He couldn't ignore her. There was too much he wanted to say:

"Hey," he reluctantly opened.

"Where are you?"

"James Madison Park."

"Can I join you?" She seemed defeated.

"You can. Is everything okay?"

"No. I'll explain when I get there."

"Okay. I'm on the same bench as last time."

"I'll be there in fifteen minutes." Ambivalence, not hatred or joy, was the overwhelming emotion. He continued his gaze over the darkening water, a fiery explosion between it and the heavens above. The Tissot read 6:55PM. Assuming she stuck to her timeline, she'd be there by 7:10PM. He looked down at the ticking sliver frequently in anticipation. Soon, it ticked over to the anticipated time. He shifted, his positioning such that his torso was now perpendicular to the bank. No headlights. He shifted back to his original position, worried his anticipation jinxed the opportunity. More ticks passed, then, in the corner of his left eye, he noticed a pair of lights streak over the lake, stop, then pivot away counterclockwise.

Again he shifted. This time, the site was the one he anticipated, although the glamorous blouse ensemble was now a loose hoody over a pair of leggings, the color of both indiscernible in the low light. He waved to direct her, watching anxiously as she crossed the lawn.

"Hi," he uttered. She tightly wrapped her arms around his waist. He followed suit. Nothing was said.

"Hi," she finally replied. Thin lines of mascara shot from the corner of each eye.

"Come sit." They sat on the cooling metal planks. "What's going on?"

"Neil and I are done."

"How'd that happen?"

"After you left we got into an argument because he thought it was a mistake to invite you to Double U. He thought I was toying with you."

"How so?"

"I don't know. I genuinely thought you guys were having a good time and that it would've been okay to bring you along. He clearly didn't."

"I see."

"It went to shit after that. I don't even remember what we said." She began sniffling. "I don't know. What do you think?"

"Think about what?"

"Do you think I made a mistake?"

"Do you think you made a mistake?"

"Now's not the time for one of your psychological mindfucks Theo."

"It's not a mindfuck. Why do you think you made a mistake?" She settled into the bench, then remained silent for several moments.

"Because I cheated on Tyler with him." His posture was undeterred, though the revelation deeply shook him.

"When did this happen?"

"Last summer, immediately after he left for the airport."

"That night?"

"Yes, and almost every night that summer. We kept it a secret. I should've known better. Neil was always around us. For the longest time I assumed it was because they were best friends. Come to find out he hadn't liked Tyler for years."

"You and Tyler were only together for four."

"Exactly. He thought he was unstable, and that I was too good for him. He wasn't wrong." She shrugged with a forced smile. He smiled back in respect of her elegant recounting of the crooked psychological saga. "Anyway, his plan was to wait until Tyler messed up, which he did, before making a move, which he did. What he didn't do was tell me he'd be studying abroad in the fall. Well, tell me at an appropriate time."

"When did he tell you?"

"Two days before he left for Paris. Fucking idiot."

"So he told you all of this? And yet he still managed to capture your heart?"

"He's hard to say no to. And even when you do, he doesn't take it for an answer. He brought me cookies on Christmas Eve, then came by a few more times after Christmas, each instance being more charming than the last, each one planting a seed about what a piece of shit Tyler was. But he didn't ask me out until a few weeks ago. I told him no. That's when he told me everything about the last four years: how he viewed me from afar, how jealous he was, and how he wanted nothing more than a chance at a relationship. I then said yes." He again remained upright, though now maintaining his stoicism was exponentially more difficult. Not because of her story, but because the story exposed a disturbing truth – he and the masterpiece embarked on the same romantic conquest, leveraging the same volatile quarterback as a trojan horse. Despite their radical differences, they were identical at their cores. Rabid chimps warring for the same territory.

"Wow. That's a lot." The comment applied to both him and her.

"I know. That's why I came to you. I knew you would listen. I greatly appreciate you for that." She set her hand daintily on his thigh. He glanced down, then turned towards the lake to witness the day's last embers peeking through Picnic Point's blooming trees, their branches swaying in the dying wind. She'd moved closer, exactly how he envisioned the scene unfolding. That scene, however, had lost its luster, much like the movie he'd been acting out with her since they met. He didn't resent her, far from, but she represented his past. His future lied in the boundless fading horizon, in the countless stars above them, in the stories yet to be told.

"And I appreciate you thinking of me in that way. Let's get you home." She nodded. They walked towards the parking lot where, a few minutes later, a white Accord arrived. They waved goodbye emotionlessly, though underneath the surface their respective tumults continued, imparting seeds of greater violence to be unleashed far into the future.

XXX

Throughout Madison spring had emerged from its extended hibernation. The forceful southern winds shifted to the opposite pole, their temperate brother now presiding over the blossoming flowers and vibrant vegetation. When the Class of 2015 graduated on Saturday, May 16th, the gloomy winter was nothing more than a statistic in the meteorological record book as Katie Couric sent thousands of matte black and cardinal gowned graduates into a daunting new world amongst a rousing crowd of cheerful families. To him, it was merely a busy weekend of apparel pushing.

Apart from these hectic few days, it'd been a productive time. He'd read through the novel three more times, each instance unlocking a better story than the last along with ever more petty grammatical errors. Editing while at the store proved to be easier than writing, affording him more time in the evenings. He started going to the gym after work and resumed running down the Lakeshore Path, an activity he greatly enjoyed last summer. His routine and surroundings once again invigorated him, and he looked forward to another peaceful and productive summer.

The only imperfection was the lack of feedback he'd received from the few with which he shared the novel. The sole person who'd given feedback was Eliza, and she'd only read an incomplete first draft. From the others – his younger sister, Jared, Kristoff, and Hank's girlfriend Hannah – he'd received nothing. Their opinions were necessary, the harsher the better. Too much sacrifice had been made to be no better than a hobbyist.

As for him and Eliza, they hadn't seen each other since that evening at James Madison Park. They kept tabs on one another through short correspondences and occasionally through Jared. She'd finished two of her five courses from last semester and looked forward to completing the other three in anticipation of returning to school full-time in the fall. It would be a challenging few months, but she was prepared, determined to regain the fire she left scattered throughout her mangled apartment. As for the beast who mangled it, his 15 year rot was in its infant stages.

He turned onto Langdon St. the Monday following graduation to a fantastic site. The Greeks were gone apart from the final stragglers shoving their rabid furniture into the back of U-Hauls with help from their parents, who were often perplexed by the damage. The trees above rustled as the warm southern wind, as Frank said, continued to blow in from across the sea, lingering in the morning air. State St. was equally tranquil apart from the occasional tourist photographing the Capitol. After the routine detour to Stop & Shop, he too basked in the iconic site: the rising sun staged to the dome's upper left, perched on layered stratus shelves made golden by their constituent whose unsuppressed beams peppered State St. with shadows of the buildings and foliage captivating those walking below. It was a timeless reminder of the unmistakable beauty that was Madison, WI.

Almost every morning he was afforded the same picturesque site, the only variation coming on Sundays when he'd walk to the Lounge first and confirm the shrink's staunch ritual. As expected, he never faltered, always seated at the third table adjacent to the window in the easterly-facing aisle seat opposite a 11" x 14" water stain. The sight always made him stop briefly and smile before walking to the store.

May and June proved as relaxing and surreal as those of last year. However, come July, reality began to creep in. His lease was up and Derrick, Hank, Kai, and Brody had managed to secure new accommodations in the spring. It was inevitable. They were going into their senior years and wanted to live with a smaller number of their fellow classmates. He didn't blame them, though he believed he'd shown enough maturity to at least warrant an offer. As for the group upstairs, they'd already made plans to move closer to campus, a fact he discovered while helping Seth move out. The sting from this abandonment was less severe, but it still compounded, and again reminded him of the sacrifices necessary to do what he'd done the past nine months.

A lifeline soon came. The building next door, 112 Langdon St., had a vacancy. It was a fine space: narrow, but with a sizable living room containing a Carolina blue suede couch and metal barstools, a gally kitchen, and a spacious bedroom with a large maple-veneered closet and beige-tiled on-suite. Best of all, it'd be all his. It would be more expensive, $700/mo. as opposed to $600/mo., but he could afford the difference, at least for a few months.

With August fast approaching, the pressure mounted to finish and distribute the book. It now had a title – Forward, A Madison Story – but no cover, no summary, and nobody who could bring it to the masses. His days became less centered around writing the novel and more about selling it. Most writing now consisted of pedantically emailing prospective publishers and printers asking for prices. 35 publishers replied "no", and 12 printers gave him prices that'd only be reasonable if he slept in the 944's trunk. Apparently this stage is when artists began to starve.

August 1st came earlier than expected. He woke up at 3:00AM to a railroad spike jammed in the left side of his skull. The pain was beyond anything he'd experienced before. He rose and paced around the apartment. No relief. He lied back down, rolling from side to side hoping to fall asleep. Still no relief. As he lay still, the spike induced a nauseating hoarse cough, leading him to crawl over the porcelain goddess and adorn her with vile saliva. He immediately began to fear this migraine was something far more dangerous, even deadly. In a final salvo to self-medicate, he headed towards Stop & Shop. Upon his arrival, he frantically asked the clerk for Extra Strength Aleve before snatching a white Ultra Monster, both of which he cracked open immediately after the clerk returned his credit card. Barely two steps outside the door, he started an ominous 30 minute timer.

BAAAP BAAAP BAAAP

He slowly rotated his torso to silence the pedantic blaring. Now that it stopped, he returned to his slumber, the spike vanquished. "Thank fucking God." He rose a few hours later and went about his morning like always, with one exception:

Hey, I could use a fantastic idea generator. Are you doing anything for dinner tonight?

What kind of ideas?

Ideas for how to publish my book and not become homeless in the process.

I may have some. Forage at 7?

Wonderful. See you then. Thank you Eliza.

The day was spent making slight alterations to the cover: a faded upshot of the Capitol resembling the view he had that November night with *Wisconsin* highlighted in gold along with the "Forward" title and "A Madison Story" subtext, his pen name "K. W. Roberts" at the bottom. It wasn't glamourous, but much like the contents it was romantic and sincere. He darkened the gold slightly, then gratifyingly gestured like an Italian sculptor admiring his perfected work. All components had now been analyzed, chastised, critiqued, reworked, and whittled to perfection. All that remained was to piece them together.

She arrived at Forage on time. After pleasantries were exchanged and the first few bites of bowl were downed, she cut straight to the point, as always:

"I think you should consider self-publishing."

"How would I go about that?"

"There are companies that'll print your books and let you deal with the marketing and distribution. I think you should start with a few dozen copies, give them away, let people read, then allow it to grow organically. It's more investment up front, but you control the process, and you also don't run the risk of losing rights to your book." He was impressed by her diligence. "I got a few quotes for you to compare prices – they're all approximately $600 for 50 copies. That seems to standard for this quantity."

"I'm astonished." He was, though his expression poorly masked his ambivalence.

"What's wrong?"

"Nothing."

"Your face says otherwise."

"This is almost a month's rent at my new apartment. Obviously I knew it was going to be expensive, it just didn't hit me until now."

"I get it." Silence ensued, the aroma of chickpeas and kale replaced by something far more bitter. "And that's why I want to pay for this..."

"...I couldn't ask you to do that Eliza."

"Let me finish. I'll pay for this first run, you'll pay for the subsequent ones, and I'll take a dollar royalty off each book until I recoup my money."

"That's quite an offer. But I still can't let you do that."

"Why not? I know you'll pay it back."

"It's not that. It's just..."

"...It's just you're too prideful to accept help." He froze, leaving a spoonful of red pepper hummus and kale suspended six inches above the bowl. "I know exactly what you're going to say. You want to be the master of your own kingdom. You want to do it with no help like you claim your dad and grandfather did, which is bullshit by the way. And finally, you want to prove to everybody you're worthy." She froze, a sinister leer now piercing him. "For once in your life Theo, get out of your own way."

He set down his fork and wiped his mouth. She was right. In the same breath as he'd come this far on his own was the undeniable truth he couldn't go any further without help. He stared at the opposite table edge, his life's failures playing against the varnished slate, a horrific compilation of what he knew would come if he left her brilliant ideas unrealized. Hell.

"Let's do it." They shook hands, and the evening proceeded. They met every night for the next week ironing out every detail from the binding adhesive to the future price points for 100, 250, and 1000 copies. A proof was printed on Thursday. It rendered him speechless, leaving a dime-sized stain in the center right crease on page 195. All that remained was to pick up the first order the following Saturday.

7:00PM struck, the anticipation finally over. He sped out the store, quickly locking the door before jogging towards his car parked on Lakelawn Place, a side street situated halfway between Langdon St. and Lake Mendota. He pulled out of the lot and headed due west towards her house in Middleton Hills. There was only one appropriate song to capture the moment – My Way.

He arrived 20 minutes later. She stood on her elm-lined driveway, a two foot cardboard cube at her feet.

"Well how about that!"

"Yeah, how about it," she answered whilst handing him a carbon handle switchblade. "You do the honors." He took it and meticulously ran the stainless steel blade through the packaging, effortlessly dismantling it like a neurotic coroner. Inside lay five perfect rows of ten volumes sandwiched between crumpled brown craft paper. After adoring the site for a few seconds, he grabbed a volume from the third row and opened the front cover. With a black felt-tip marker from his right pocket he began writing:

Eliza,

Thank you for believing in me. I hope you continue to leave me without words.

Theo

He handed it to her. She accepted it and graciously read the note, letting out a sigh from underneath an appreciative smile. "You'll never be without words." She then gestured toward the house. "Let's celebrate."

"Let's!" They went inside through the walkout basement adjacent to the garage. The basement was awash with plush camel carpet and blue grey walls, a beige suede couch facing a TV on the left wall. The opposite wall was covered by a masterpiece of oak, granite, and emerald stained glass, in front of which lay an equally impressive harvest stained pool table crafted in such an impressive manner it appeared milled from a fallen trunk. She opened one of the oak panels to retrieve two champagne coupes, and another underneath to retrieve their chilled constituent.

POP

"To the next Hemingway!" She toasted.

"And the only K. W. Roberts!"

"Shall we shoot some pool?"

"I think that can be arranged. But first..."

"They call you Lady Luck. But there is room for doubt. At times you have a very unlady-like way of running out."

He swung around the cue swaying to Frank's intro. He didn't know it yet, but tonight, all the luck was with him.

The soft dawn cracked open their eyes revealing a smile on each of their faces. "Good morning." She sat up on the middle cushion while he propped himself on his elbows:

"Good morning." He checked his watch. 7:05AM. "I really should get going."

"You don't want breakfast?"

"Another time. I need to meet a friend."

"Is this friend going to get a copy."

"He will. I promised him one."

"I hope he appreciates it."

"He will."

"I'll talk to you later." They kissed.

Any other day he would've disappeared with her into the caressing fabric, but this was one patron he would never keep waiting. After sneaking through the backyard, he quickly loaded the box into the 944's trunk and sped through the wooded drive, the fortress of elm trees shading the morning sun, the few penetrating beams illuminating the interior's worn leather. He arrived just in time. 7:57AM. Parking the 944 underneath College Library, he snatched a copy from the middle row and sprinted towards Memorial Union, entering from the west and continuing towards the Lounge. He found the water stained table and sat down in the west facing aisle seat. 8:03AM.

He waited. 8:33AM. 9:17AM. 10:03AM. The patron remained absent. He grazed the elevated matte letters of the cover, each peak rendering a smile, each valley another. Though the patron's broken promise soured his expression, it quickly returned to a genial grin as he realized he kept his. Not only those to himself, but to all, including those who only occupied his dreams.

As he turned to leave, he ran his thumb across the title one more time. Two words then violently struck him – backward, beyond. He grabbed a napkin from the adjacent table and scribbled the words with the marker in his pocket. The trilogy was set...

The Locations of Forward

The Locations of Forward – Madison West

Porter Boathouse – 680 Babcock Dr.

Theo's Dorm (Dejope Residence Hall) – 640 Elm Dr.

UW Health University Hospital – 600 Highland Ave.

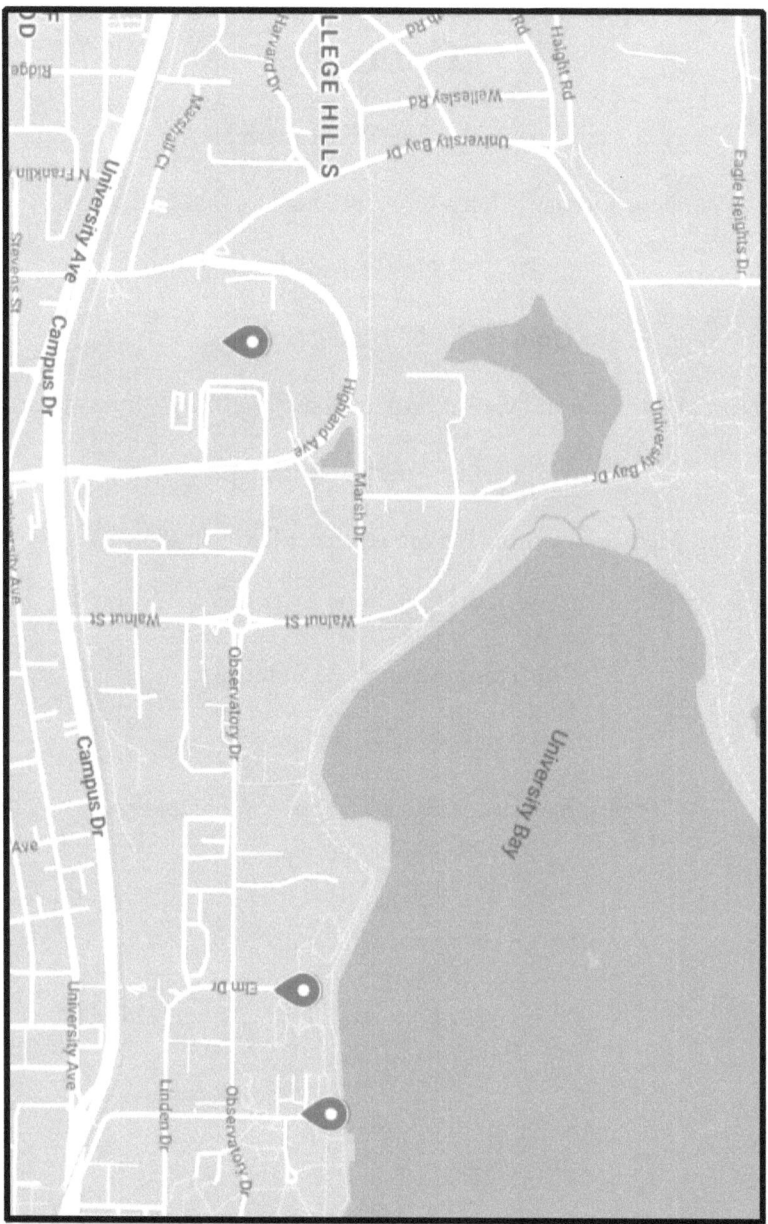

The Locations of Forward – Madison Central

Chaser's* – 339 W. Gorham St.

College Library (Helen C. White Hall) – 600 N Park St.

Cyc* – 773 University Ave. #205

Double U – 620 University Ave.

Eliza's Dorm (Grand Central Apartments) – 1022 W Johnson St.

Forage – 665 State St.

Memorial Union*Union Terrace – 800 Langdon St.

Stop & Shop – 501 State St.

The Sconnie Store*- 515 State St.

Theo's Apartment – 104 Langdon St.

Theo's Favorite Sandwich Shop – 564 State St.

*Location has changed and*or business has closed.*

The Locations of Forward – Madison East

James Madison Park – 614 E Gorham St.

Old Edgewater Hotel – 1001 Wisconsin Pl.

The Statehouse (Inside New Edgewater Hotel) – 1001 Wisconsin Pl.

Wisconsin Statue, Capitol Building – 2 E Main St.

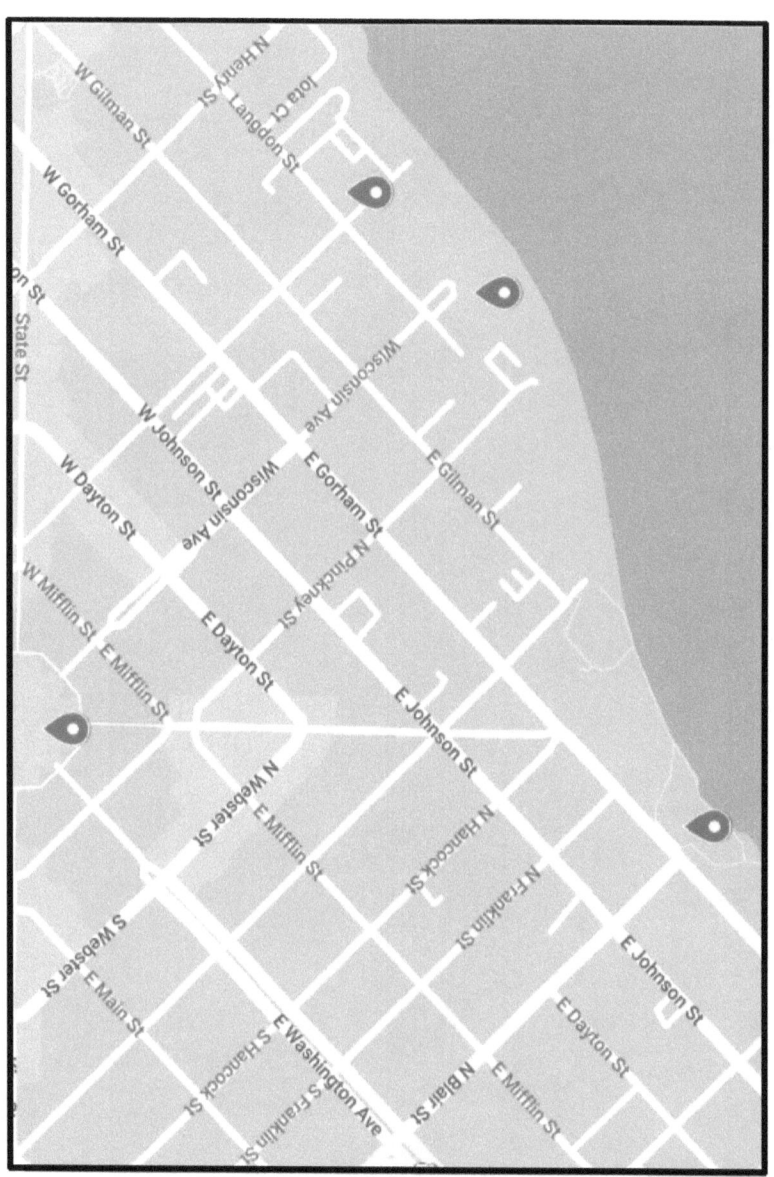

www.ingramcontent.com/pod-product-compliance
Lightning Source LLC
Chambersburg PA
CBHW032115020726
47494CB00007BA/2077